"Give That Back."

Lilah made a lunge for the pad. Zane evaded her reach.

"Why do you need it so badly?"

"Those sketches are…private."

He handed her the pad, but used it to draw her closer.

The relief that had spiraled through her when she thought he hadn't checked out the drawings dissolved. "You *looked*."

"Uh-huh." He drew her close enough that her thighs brushed his and the sketch pad, which she was clutching like a shield, was flattened between them.

"And you would be drawing and painting me because…?"

Lilah briefly closed her eyes. "You saw the painting in my apartment."

"Because then you could avoid admitting that you're attracted to me. And have been ever since we met two years ago."

Gently, he eased the sketch pad from her grip. "You don't need that anymore." He tossed the pad aside. "Not when you have the real thing."

Dear Reader,

The final story of The Pearl House trilogy centers on two people who have deep issues with relationships and wildly opposing agendas. Both Lilah Cole and Zane Atraeus are a little extreme by nature, but with some very likable quirks.

Desperate to escape the embarrassment and undeserved notoriety of being her billionaire boss's dumped date, all Lilah wants is to put that mistake behind her and get back on track with achieving her five-year marriage plan. Until she runs headlong into the object of her secret fantasies for the past two years, the dark and dangerously unreliable Zane Atraeus.

As powerfully attracted as Zane is to Lilah, he has trust issues with women who are on the hunt for well-heeled husbands, although he is fascinated and drawn by her methodical approach and, actually, just can't seem to leave her alone.

Short term is Zane's middle name, but as time goes by, he finds himself wanting to convince Lilah that despite his terrible track record with commitment, he just could be the perfect man for her....

I hope you find when you read it, that I really did have the most fun writing Lilah and Zane!

Fiona

FIONA BRAND

A PERFECT HUSBAND

HARLEQUIN®

entertain, enrich, inspire™

Recycling programs
for this product may
not exist in your area.

ISBN-13: 978-0-373-73191-6

A PERFECT HUSBAND

www.Harlequin.com

Printed in U.S.A.

Books by Fiona Brand

Harlequin Desire

*A Breathless Bride #2154
*A Tangled Affair #2166
*A Perfect Husband #2178

Silhouette Romantic Suspense

Cullen's Bride #914
Heart of Midnight #977
Blade's Lady #1023
Marrying McCabe #1099
Gabriel West: Still the One #1219
High-Stakes Bride #1403

Silhouette Books

Sheiks of Summer
   "Kismet"

*The Pearl House

Other titles by this author available in ebook format.

FIONA BRAND

lives in the sunny Bay of Islands, New Zealand. Now that both her sons are grown, she continues to love writing books and gardening. After a life-changing time in which she met Christ, she has undertaken study for a bachelor of theology and has become a member of The Order of St. Luke, Christ's healing ministry.

For the Lord. Thank you.

Each of the gates is a single pearl, and the
street of the city is pure gold, transparent as glass.
—*Revelation* 21:21

One

Dark hair twisted in a sleek, classic knot... Exotic eyes the shifting colors of the sea... A delicate curvy body that made him burn from the inside out...

A sharp rapping on the door of his Sydney hotel suite jerked Zane Atraeus out of a restless, dream-tossed sleep. Shielding his eyes from the glare of the morning sun, he shoved free of the huge silk-draped confection of a bed he'd collapsed into some time short of four that morning.

Pulling on the jeans he'd tossed over a chair, he dragged jet-lagged fingers through his tangled hair and padded to the door.

Memory punched back. An email Zane had found confirming that his half brother Lucas had purchased an engagement ring for a woman Zane could have sworn Lucas barely knew. *Lilah Cole: the woman Zane had secretly wanted for two years and had denied himself.*

His temper, which had been running on a short fuse ever since he had learned that not only was Lucas dating Lilah, he was planning on *marrying* her, ignited as he took in glittering chandeliers and turquoise-and-gold furnishings.

The overstuffed opulence was a far cry from the exotic but spare Mediterranean decor of his island home, Medinos. Instead of soothing him, the antiques and heavily swagged drapes only served to remind him that he had not been born to any of this. He would have to have a word with his new personal assistant, who clearly had a romantic streak.

Halfway across the sitting room the unmistakable sound of the front door lock disengaging made him stiffen.

Lucas Atraeus stepped into the room. Zane let out a self-deprecating breath.

Ten years ago, in L.A., it would have been someone breaking in, but this was Australia and his father's company, the mega wealthy Atraeus Group, owned the hotel so, of course, Lucas had gotten a key. "Ever heard of a phone?"

Closing the door behind him, Lucas tossed a key card down on the hall table. "I phoned, you didn't answer. Remember Lilah?"

The reason Zane was in Sydney instead of in Florida doing his job as the company "fixer" and closing a crucial land deal that had balanced on a knife's edge for the past week? "Your new fiancée." The tantalizing beauty who had almost snared him into a reckless night of passion two years ago. "Yeah, I remember."

Lucas looked annoyed. "I haven't asked her yet. How did you find out?"

Zane's jaw tightened at the confirmation. "My new P.A. was your old P.A., remember?" Which was why Zane had chanced across the internet receipt for Lucas's latest purchase. Apparently Elena was still performing the role of personal shopper for his brother in her spare time.

"Ahh. Elena." He glanced around the room. Comprehension gleamed in his eyes.

Now definitely in a bad mood, Zane turned on his heel and strolled in the direction of the suite's kitchenette. A large ornately gilded mirror threw his reflection back at him—darkly tanned skin, broad shoulders and a lean, muscled torso bisected by a tracery of scars. Three silver studs, the reminder of a misspent youth, glinted in one ear.

In the lavish elegance of the suite, he looked uncivilized, barbaric and faintly sinister, as different from his two classically handsome half brothers as the proverbial chalk was from cheese. Not something he had ever been able to help with the genes he'd inherited from the rough Salvatore side of his family, and the inner scars he had developed as a homeless kid roaming the streets of L.A.

He found a glass, filled it with water from the dispenser in the fridge door and drank in long, smooth swallows. The cold water failed to douse the intense, unreasoning jealousy that seared him every time he thought of Lucas and Lilah, the picture-perfect couple.

An engagement.

His reaction to the idea was as fierce and surprising as it had been when he had discovered Elena admiring a picture of the engagement ring.

The empty glass hit the kitchen counter with a controlled click. "I didn't think Lilah was your type."

As gorgeous and ladylike as Ambrosi Pearls's head jewelry designer was, in Zane's opinion, Lilah was too efficiently, calculatingly focused on hunting for a well-heeled husband.

Two years ago, when they had first met at the annual ball of a charity for homeless children—of which he was the patron—he had witnessed the smooth way Lilah had targeted her escort's wealthy boss. Even armored by the formidable depth of betrayal in his past, Zane had been oddly entranced by the businesslike gleam in her eyes. He had not been able to resist the temptation to rescue the hapless older man and spoil her pitch.

Unfortunately, things had gotten out of hand when he and Lilah had ended up alone in a private reception room and he had given into temptation and kissed her. One kiss had led to another, sparking a conflagration that had threatened to engulf them both. Given that he had been irritated by Lilah's agenda, that she was not the kind of woman he was usually attracted to, his loss of control still perplexed him. If his previous personal assistant hadn't found them at a critical moment, he would have made a very big mistake.

Lucas, who had followed him into the kitchen, scribbled a number on the back of a business card and left it on the counter. "Lilah has agreed to be my date at Constantine's wedding. I'm leaving for Medinos in a couple of hours. I was going to arrange for her to fly in the day before the wedding, but since you're here—" Lucas frowned. "By the way, why are you here? I thought you were locked into negotiations."

"I'm taking a couple of days." A muscle pulsed along Zane's jaw.

Lucas shrugged and opened the fridge door.

The shelves were packed with an array of fresh fruit, cheeses, pâtés and juices. Absently, Zane noted his assistant had also stocked the fridge with chocolate-dipped strawberries.

"Good move." Lucas examined a bottle of very expensive French champagne then replaced it. "Nothing like making the vendor think we're cooling off to fast-track a sale. Mind if I have something to eat? I missed breakfast."

Probably too busy shuttling between women to think about food. The last Zane had heard Lucas had also been having a wild "secret" affair with Carla Ambrosi, the public relations officer for Ambrosi and the sister of the woman their brother, Constantine, was marrying.

"Oysters." Lucas lifted a brow. "Having someone in?"

Zane stared grimly at the platter of oysters on the half shell, complete with rock salt and lemon wedges. "Not as far as I know."

Unless his new assistant had made some arrangement.

If she was helping Lucas with his engagement during her

lunch breaks, anything was possible. "Help yourself to the food, the juice…"

My girl.

The thought welled up out of the murk of his subconscious and slipped neatly past all of the reasons that commitment could never work for him. Especially, with a woman like Lilah.

Since the age of nine, relationships had been a difficult area.

After being abandoned by his extravagant, debt-ridden mother on a number of occasions while she had flitted from marriage to marriage, he had definite trust issues with women, especially those on the hunt for wealthy husbands.

Marriage was out.

Lucas took out the bowl of strawberries and surveyed the tempting fruit.

"It doesn't bother you that Lilah's on the hunt for a husband?"

An odd expression flitted across Lucas's face. "Actually, I respect her straightforward approach. It's refreshing."

Despite every attempt to relax, Zane's fingers curled into fists. *So Lucas had fallen under her spell, too.*

Try as he might, now that Zane had acknowledged that Lilah was his, he could not dismiss the thought. With every second that passed, the concept became more and more stubbornly real.

It was a fact that for the two years following the incendiary passion that had almost ended in lovemaking, he had been tormented by the knowledge that Lilah could have been his.

He had controlled the desire to have a reckless fling with Lilah. He had controlled himself.

Lucas selected the largest, plumpest strawberry. "Lilah has a fear of flying. I was hoping, since you're piloting the company jet that you could take her with you to Medinos when you leave."

Zane's jaw tightened. Everything in him rejected Lucas's

easy assertion that Zane would tamely fall into place and
hand-deliver Lilah to his bed.

He fixed on the first part of Lucas's statement. In all the
time he had known Lilah she had never told *him* she had a fear
of flying. Somehow that fact was profoundly irritating. "Just
out of curiosity, how long have you known Lilah?" Lucas did
spend time in Sydney, but not as much as Zane. He had never
heard Lilah so much as mention Lucas's name.

"A week, give or take."

Zane went still inside. He knew his brother's schedule.
They had all had to adjust their plans when Roberto Ambrosi,
a member of a once-powerful and wealthy Medinian family, had died. The Atraeus Group had been forced to protect
its interests by moving on the almost bankrupted Ambrosi
Pearls. A hostile takeover to recover huge debts racked up
by Roberto had been averted when Constantine had stunned
them all by resurrecting his engagement to Sienna Ambrosi.
The impending marriage had gone a long way toward healing the acrimonious rift that had developed between the two
families when Roberto had leveraged money on the basis of
the first engagement.

He knew that, apart from a couple of flying visits in the
last couple of weeks—one to attend Roberto's funeral—that
Lucas had been committed offshore. He had only arrived in
Sydney the previous day.

Zane had spent most of the previous week in Sydney in
order to attend the annual general meeting of the charity. As
usual, Lilah, who helped out with the art auctions, had been
polite, reserved, the tantalizing, high-priced sensuality that
was clearly reserved for the future Mr. Cole on ice. She had
not mentioned Lucas. "Why not take Lilah with *you?*"

Lucas seemed inordinately interested in selecting a second
strawberry. "It's a gray area."

Realization dawned. Lilah had not been subtle about her
quest of finding a husband. He had just never seen Lucas as
a candidate for an arranged marriage. "This is a first date."

A trace of emotion flickered in Lucas's gaze. "I needed someone on short notice. As it happens, after running a background check, I think Lilah is perfect for me. She's talented, attractive, she's got a good business head on her shoulders, she's even a—"

"What about Carla?"

Lucas dropped the ripe berry as if it had seared his fingertips.

The final piece of the puzzle fell into place. Zane realized what the odd look in Lucas's eyes had been just moments ago: desperation. Hot outrage surged through him. "You're still involved with Carla."

"How did you know? No, don't tell me. Elena." Lucas put the bowl of strawberries back in the fridge and closed the door. "Carla and I are over."

But only just.

Suddenly the instant relationship with Lilah made sense. When Sienna married Constantine, Carla would practically be family. If it came out that Lucas had been sleeping with Carla, intense pressure would be applied. Under the tough exterior, when it came to women, Lucas was vulnerable.

He was using Lilah as a buffer, insurance that Carla, who had a reputation for flamboyant scenes, would not try to publicly force him to formalize their secret affair with a marriage proposal.

That meant that love did not come into the equation.

If Lucas genuinely wanted Lilah, Zane would walk away, however that was not the case. Lucas, who had once been in the untenable position of having a girlfriend die in a car crash after they had argued about the secret abortion she'd had, was using her to avert an unpleasant situation. As calculating as Lilah was with relationships, she did not deserve to be caught in the middle of a showdown between Lucas and Carla.

Relief eased some of his fierce tension. He didn't think Lilah had had time to sleep with Lucas yet. Somehow that fact was very important. "Okay. I'll do it."

Lucas looked relieved. "You won't regret it."

Zane wasn't so sure.

He wondered if Lucas had any inkling that he had just placed a temptation Zane had doggedly resisted for over two years directly in his path.

Two

Heart pounding at the step she was taking, her first bona fide risk in twelve years of carefully managed, featureless and fruitless dating, Lilah Cole boarded the sleek private jet that belonged to Ambrosi Pearls's new owner, The Atraeus Group.

The nervy anticipation that had buoyed her as she had made her way through passport control ebbed as the pretty blonde stewardess, Jasmine, seated her.

Placing the soft white leather tote bag that went with her white jeans and comfy, oversized white shirt on the floor, Lilah dug out the discreet, white leather-bound folder she had bought with her. She had been braced for another stress-filled encounter with the dark and edgily dangerous Zane Atraeus, the youngest and wildest of the Atraeus brothers, but she was the sole occupant of the luxurious cabin.

Fifteen minutes later, with the noise from the jet engines reaching a crescendo and a curtain of gray rain blotting out much of the view from her tiny window, Lilah was still the only passenger.

She squashed the ridiculous idea that she was in any way disappointed as she fastened her seat belt with fingers that were not entirely steady.

Flying was not her favorite pastime; she was not a natural risk taker. Like her approach to relationships, she preferred to keep her feet on the ground. A stubborn part of her brain couldn't ignore the concept of all that space between the aircraft and the earth's surface. To compound the problem, the weather forecast was for violent thunder and lightning.

As the jet taxied through the sweeping rain, Lilah ignored the in-flight safety video and concentrated on the one thing she *could* control. Flipping open the folder, she studied the profiles she had compiled.

Cole women had a notorious record for falling victim to the *coup de foudre*—the clap of thunder—for falling passionately and disastrously for the wrong man then literally being left holding the baby. Aware that she possessed the same creative, passionate streak that ran through both her artistic and bohemian mother and grandmother, Lilah had developed a system for avoiding The Mistake.

It was a blueprint for long-term happiness, a wedding plan. She had found that writing down the steps she needed to take to achieve the relationship she wanted somehow demystified the whole process, making it seem not such a leap in the dark.

When she did eventually give herself to a man, she was confident it would be in a committed relationship, not some wild fling. She wanted marriage, babies, the stable, controlled environment she had craved as a child.

She was determined that any children she had would have two loving parents, not one stressed and strained beyond her limits.

Over the last three years, despite interviewing an exhaustive number of candidates, she had not managed to find a man who met her marriage criteria and appealed to her on the all-important physical level. Scent in particular had proved to be a formidable barrier to identifying someone with whom she could have an intimate relationship. It was not that the men she had interviewed had smelled bad, just that in some subtle way they had not smelled *right*. However, things were finally taking a positive turn.

Lilah studied the notes she had made on her new boss, Lucas Atraeus, and a small number of other men, and the points system she had developed based on a matchmaking website's recommendations. She spent an enjoyable few minutes reviewing Lucas's good points.

On paper he was the most perfect man she had ever met. He was electrifyingly good-looking and used a light cologne that she didn't mind. He possessed the kind of dark, dangerous features that had proved to be an unfortunate weakness of hers and yet, in terms of a future husband, he ticked every box of her list.

For the first time she had found a man who was her type and yet he was safe, steady, reliable. The situation was a definite win-win.

She should be thrilled that he had asked her to a family wedding. This date, despite its risky nature, was the most positive she'd had in years and, at the age of twenty-nine, her biological clock was ticking.

She didn't know Lucas well. They had only met in the context of work over the past few days, with a "business" lunch at a nearby cafe tossed in, during which he had told her that not only did he need an escort for his brother's wedding, but that he was looking for a relationship with a view to marriage.

Like her, she didn't think Lucas had succumbed to any kind of intense physical attraction. He preferred to take a more measured approach.

If it were possible to control her emotions and fall in love with Lucas, she had already decided she would do it.

She checked her watch and frowned. They were leaving a little earlier than scheduled. If the pilot had only waited a few more minutes, Zane might have made it.

She squashed another whisper of disappointment and

snapped the window shutter closed. Witnessing the small jet launching itself into the dark, turbulent center of the storm was something she did not need to see.

The liftoff was bumpy. During the steep ascent, wind buffeted the jet and lightning flickered through the other windows of the cabin. When they finally leveled out, Lilah's nerves were stretched taut. She had taken a sedative before she had left her apartment, but so far it had failed to have any effect.

The stewardess, who had retreated to a separate compartment, reappeared and offered her a drink. With the cabin to herself, sleeping seemed the best option, so Lilah took another sedative. According to her doctor, one should have worked; two would definitely knock her out.

She was rereading Lucas's compatibility quotient, which was extremely high, her lids drooping, when a heavy crack of thunder shook the small jet. Lightning flashed. In that instant the door to the cockpit popped open. Zane Atraeus, tall, sleekly broad-shouldered and dressed in somber black, was framed in the searing flicker of light.

The jet lurched; the folder flew off her lap. The clasp sprang open as it hit the floor, scattering loose sheets. Lilah barely noticed. As always, her artist's eye was riveted. Zane's golden skin and chiseled face—which she had shamelessly, secretly, painted for the past two years—could have been lifted straight out of a Dalmasio oil. Even the imperfections, the subversive glint of the studs in his lobe, the faint disruption to the line of his nose, as if it had once been broken, were somehow… perfect.

She blinked as Zane strolled toward her. Her vision readjusted to the warm glow of the cabin lights. Until Zane had moved, she had not been entirely convinced that he was real. She thought she could have been caught up in one of the vivid, unsettling dreams that had disturbed her sleep ever since The Regrettable Episode two years ago.

Unlike the temporary effect of the lightning flash on her

vision, the events of that night had been indelibly seared into her consciousness. "I thought you missed the flight."

His steady dark gaze made her stomach tighten. "I never miss when I'm the pilot."

Aware that the contents of the folder had spilled into the aisle, and that the topmost sheet which held the glaringly large title, *The Wedding Plan,* was clearly visible, Lilah lunged forward in an attempt to regather the incriminating sheets. Her seat belt held her pinned. By the time she had the buckle unfastened, Zane had collected both the folder and the loose sheets.

Her cheeks burned as he straightened. She was certain he had read some of the contents, enough to get the gist of what they were about. She took the sheets and stuffed them back into the folder. "I didn't know you could fly."

"It's not something I advertise."

Unlike the lavish parties he regularly attended and the endless stream of gorgeous models he escorted. Although, flying did fit with his love of extreme sports: diving, kitesurfing and snowboarding, to name a few. Zane had a well-publicized love for anything that involved adrenaline.

It occurred to Lilah, as she jammed the folder in her tote bag, out of sight, that she didn't know what Lucas liked to do in his spare time. She must make the effort to find out.

Zane shrugged out of his jacket and tossed it over the arm of the seat across the aisle. "How long have you been afraid of flying?"

Lilah tore her gaze from the snug fit of his black T-shirt and the muscular swell of tanned biceps. She was certain that beyond an intoxicating whiff of sandalwood she could detect the scent of his skin.

Her blush deepened as she was momentarily flung back to the night of The Episode. Zane had suggested they go to an empty reception room so they could indulge their mutual passion for art by studying the oils displayed on the walls.

She couldn't remember much about the garish abstracts. She would never forget the moment Zane had pulled her close.

The clean, masculine scent of his skin and the exotic undernote of sandalwood had filled her nostrils, making her head spin. When he had kissed her, his taste had filled her mouth.

Somehow they had ended up on a wide, comfortable couch. At some point the bodice of her dress had drifted to her waist, a detail that should have alarmed her. Zane had taken one breast in his mouth and her whole body had coiled unbearably tight. She could remember clutching at his shoulders, a flash of dizzying, heated pleasure, the room shimmering out of focus.

If the door hadn't popped open at that moment and Zane's date, who was also his previous personal assistant, a gorgeous redhead called Gemma, hadn't walked in, Lilah shuddered to think what would have happened next. She had dragged her bodice up and clambered off the couch. By the time she had found her clutch, which had ended up underneath the couch, Zane had shrugged into his jacket. After a clipped good-night, he had left with Gemma.

The echoing silence after the heady, intimate passion had stung. He had not suggested they meet again, which had put The Episode in its horrifying context.

Zane had not wanted a relationship; he had just wanted an interlude. Sex. He had probably thought they had been on the verge of a one night stand, that she was *easy*.

Embarrassingly, she *had* forgotten every relationship rule she had rigidly stuck to for the twelve years she had been dating.

Zane walking out so quickly then never bothering to follow up with a telephone call or text had been a blessing. It had confirmed what she had both read about him and discovered firsthand—that no matter how attractive, he could not be trusted in a relationship. If he couldn't commit to a phone call, it was unlikely he would commit to marriage.

Another shuddering crash of thunder jerked her back to the present.

Aware that Zane was waiting for an answer, she busied herself fastening her seat belt. "I've been afraid of flying forever."

Instead of sitting where he'd slung his jacket, Zane lowered himself into the seat next to hers.

She stiffened as he pried her hand off the armrest. "What are you doing?"

His fingers curled warmly through hers. "Holding your hand. Tried-and-true remedy."

Nervous tension, along with the tingling heat of his touch, zinged through her at the skin-on-skin contact. There was something distinctly forbidden about holding hands with Zane Atraeus.

Illegitimate and wild, according to the tabloids, Zane had been the instant ruination of hundreds of women, and promised to be the ruination of even more in the future. She had the shattering firsthand knowledge of exactly how that ruination was achieved.

She flexed her fingers, but his hold didn't loosen. "Shouldn't you be in the cockpit?"

"Flight deck. There's a copilot, Spiros. He doesn't need me yet."

Her stomach clenched as she was suddenly reminded that they were twenty-eight thousand feet above the ground. "How long is the flight?"

"Twenty hours, give or take. We land in Singapore to re-fuel. If you don't like flying, why are you going to Medinos?"

Trying to arrange her future with a steady, reliable husband who would not leave her. Trying to avoid the Cole women's regrettable tendency to fall victim to the *coup de foudre*.

Her head started to swim, and it was not just the dizzying effect of the sandalwood. She remembered that she had taken two sedatives. "Trying to get a life. I'm twenty-nine."

She blinked. She was beginning to feel as if she was swimming in molasses. Had she actually told him her age?

"Twenty-nine doesn't seem so old to me."

She smothered a yawn and frowned at the defensive note in his voice.

"What did you take?"

Her lids slid closed. She gave him the name of the sedative.

"They'll knock you out. I can remember having them as a kid. After my father found me in L.A., we flew to Medinos. I was a handful. I didn't like flying, either."

Curiosity kept her on the surface of sleep, caught in the net of his deep, cool voice and fascinated by the dichotomy of his character. She had read his story on the charity website. One of the things she admired about Zane was that he happily revealed his past in order to help homeless kids.

"Put your head on my shoulder if you want."

The quiet offer sent a warning thrill through her. She considered leaning against the window, but the thought that the shutter might slide open and she would catch a view clear down to the ground was not pleasant. "No, thank you." She struggled to stay upright. "You're nicer than I thought."

"Tell me," he muttered, "I'm curious. You've known me for two years. How did you think I would be?"

Her lids flickered open. Exactly how he had been the night of the ball. Dangerous, sexy. *Hot.*

With an effort of will, she controlled her mind, which had shot off on a very wrong tangent. Zane had probably been in intimate situations with more women than he could count. She doubted he would even remember how close they had come to making love. Or that she had actually—

She cut short that disturbing thought and searched for something polite to say. As an Atraeus, Zane was one of her employers now. She would have to adjust to the new dynamic.

Her stomach tensed at a thought she had cheerfully glossed over before. If she and Lucas married, their relationship would be even closer; he would be her brother-in-law. "Uh—for a start, I didn't think you even liked me."

"Was that after what happened on the couch or before?"

The flashback to the sensations that had flooded her that night was electrifying. From the knowing gleam in Zane's gaze, she was abruptly certain he knew exactly what had happened.

Embarrassed heat warmed her cheeks. He had been lying on top of her at the time. She would be naive to consider that he had not noticed that she had lost control and actually had an orgasm.

He had to know also that if Gemma hadn't turned up dangling car keys and making them jump guiltily apart, that she had been on the verge of making an even bigger mistake. "I'm surprised you remember."

"Lucas won't marry you."

The sudden change of topic jerked her lids open. The dark fire burning in Zane's eyes almost made her forget what she was about to say. "Lucas isn't the only one with a choice."

"Choose someone else."

Lilah's heart slammed against the wall of her chest. For a split second, she'd had the crazy thought that Zane had been about to say, "Choose *me.*"

From an early age she had discovered that men liked the way she looked. Something in the slant of her eyes, the curve of her cheekbones, the shape of her mouth, spelled sexual allure. On occasion attraction had spilled over into an uncomfortable fascination, although she had never thought that Zane Atraeus would find her more than ordinarily attractive.

She dragged in a lungful of air and tried to deny the heart-pounding knowledge that behind the grim tone Zane Atraeus really did want her. "What gives you the right—?"

"This."

Zane bent toward her, his head dipped. Her pulse rate rocketed.

For two years she had tortured herself about her loss of control. Now, finally, she was being offered the chance to examine what, exactly, had gone wrong.

She caught another enticing whiff of clean skin and exotic cologne. Dimly, she noted that the concept of her ruination had receded, a dangerous sign, although she was still in control. She had time to shift in her seat. If she wanted she could turn her head—

Warm fingers gripped her chin. The pressure of his mouth on hers almost stopped her heart.

Suddenly, the electrical hum every time he looked at her coalesced into stunning truth. The double whammy of her ticking biological clock combined with prolonged celibacy was the reason she was having such a difficult time controlling her responses to Zane.

Relief surged through her. She didn't know why she hadn't thought about that two years ago. It was the logical explanation. Zane had caught her at a vulnerable moment at the charity ball. She simply hadn't had the resources to resist him.

Jerking back from the seductive softness of the kiss, Lilah gulped in air.

The experience had been so riveting that the harder she had tried to suppress the memories, the more aggressively they had surfaced—in her dreams, her painting.

She had to get a grip on herself. She could not afford to take him seriously. According to the tabloids, the youngest Atraeus brother was the dark side of the mega wealthy Atraeus family, wild and dangerous to know, the bad as opposed to the good.

Which only went to prove that her judgment when it came to men was no better than her mother's or her grandmother's before her.

A little wildly she decided that the attraction was no bigger a deal for Zane than it had been two years ago. But that didn't change the disturbing knowledge that, if anything, she was in an even more vulnerable position now. The sensations already coursing through her body had the potential to destroy the future she had mapped out for herself.

She could not let that happen.

She was strong-willed. She had steered clear of intense emotions and casual flings all of her adult life. She was not going to mess up now.

With a younger man.

Zane was twenty-four, twenty-five at most, and with no sign of tempering his fast, edgy lifestyle with the encumbrances of a wife and family. He could say what he liked about his brother, but on paper, Lucas *was* perfect. He was older, more mature, ready to commit and without the wild reputation.

Those minutes on the couch with Zane and the experience of losing control and almost giving herself to a man who had demonstrated that he did not care for her had been salutary.

She knew the danger of her weakness now. On top of the healthy sex drive that came with her Cole genes, her biological clock was ticking loudly in both ears.

The thought that Zane could make her pregnant sent a hot flash through her that momentarily welded her to the seat before she managed to dismiss the notion.

Zane was not husband material. All she had to do was ignore the magnetic power of the attraction and her raging hormones, ignore the destructive impulse to throw her wedding plan away.

And throw herself beneath Zane's naked body.

Three

After a formal family dinner at the Atraeus family's Medinian castello the following evening, Lilah excused herself from the table while coffee was being served. Lucas had left some twenty minutes earlier, during dessert. His defection had been no great surprise because through the course of the evening she had become grimly certain that he was involved with another woman.

After obtaining directions from one of the kitchen staff, she paused by the door to Lucas's private suite. Stiffening her shoulders against the chill of the Mediterranean fortress walls, she rapped on the imposing door.

Lean brown fingers manacled her wrist. "I wouldn't go in there if I were you."

Lilah spun, shocked by the deep, cool voice and the knowledge that Zane had left the dinner table and followed her.

Snatching her wrist back, she rubbed at the bare skin, which still tingled and burned from his grip.

She dragged her gaze from his overlong jet-black hair and

the trio of studs glinting in one lobe. An unwanted surge of awareness added to the tension that had gripped her ever since she had arrived at the castello that evening and seen Lucas in the arms of Carla Ambrosi.

Lucas and Carla had a short but well-publicized past, which Lilah had mistakenly believed to be invented media hype. To further complicate things, Carla was Lilah's immediate boss.

Zane indicated the closed door. "Haven't you figured it out yet? Lucas is…busy."

The startling notion that, beneath the casual facade, Zane was quietly angry was shattered by the distant sound of laughter and the tap of high heels. More guests leaving the dining table, no doubt in search of one of the castello's bathrooms.

Suddenly, the stunning risk Lilah had taken in traveling thousands of miles for a first date with an extremely wealthy man whose love life was of interest to the tabloids came back to haunt her. He had fulfilled all of the criteria of her system. Now things were going disastrously wrong.

Zane jerked his head in the direction of the approaching guests. "I take it you don't want to be discovered knocking on Lucas's bedroom door?"

A wave of embarrassed heat decimated the chill. "No."

"Finally, some sense." Zane's fingers curled around her wrist again.

The startling intimacy of the hold sent another tingling jolt through her. A split second later, heart pounding with nerves, she found herself crushed against Zane's side and flattened against the cold stone of an alcove. She inhaled, bracing herself against the effect of the sandalwood and the sudden, nervous desire to laugh.

As unpleasant as the evening had been she couldn't suppress a small thrill that Zane had come to her rescue. Now they were hiding like a couple of kids.

Zane leaned out and peered around a corner. When he settled back into place she discovered that she had missed the warmth of his body.

His dark gaze touched on hers. "What I don't get is why Lucas asked you."

Lilah stiffened at the implication that she was the last person Lucas should have asked to partner him at a family wedding.

Determinedly, she stamped on the soft core of hurt that had haunted her since she was a kid—that her illegitimate birth and the poverty of her background made her less than respectable. "You certainly know how to make a girl feel special."

He frowned. "That wasn't what I meant."

"Don't worry." She dragged her gaze free from the dangerous, too-knowing sympathy in his. "I have no problems with the reality check."

She just wished she had thought things through before she had left home. Labeled "Catch of the Year" in a prominent women's magazine, Lucas *had* been too good to be true.

Somewhere in the distance a door snapped shut, cutting off the sound of footsteps and laughter. The abrupt return to silence made Lilah doubly aware of the masculine heat emanating from Zane's body and that the pale pearlized silk of her gown suddenly seemed too thin, the scooped neckline too revealing.

Hot color flooded her cheeks as the stressed uncertainty that had driven her to go in search of Lucas, and the truth, gave way to the searing memory of the kiss on the flight out.

The sedatives she had taken had kicked in shortly afterward. She had not seen Zane again until they had landed in Singapore, where two more passengers, clients of The Atraeus Group, had boarded the jet. Courtesy of the extra passengers, the rest of the flight had been uneventful. During the customs procedures, aware that Zane had been keeping tabs on her, she had managed to separate herself from him and had taken a taxi to her hotel.

Zane checked the corridor again. "All clear, and your reputation intact."

"Unfortunately, my reputation is already shredded."

That was the risk she had accepted in traveling thousands of miles on a first date with her billionaire boss. She hadn't yet had time to formulate the full extent of the damage this would do to her marriage plan. Her only hope was that the other men on her list didn't read the gutter press.

Jaw locked, she marched to the door of Lucas's suite and rapped again.

Zane leaned one broad shoulder against the door frame, arms folded across his chest. "You don't give up easily, do you?"

Lilah tried not to notice the way the dim light of an antique wall lamp flared across his taut, molded cheekbones, the tough line of his jaw. "I prefer the direct approach."

"Just remember I tried to save you."

The door eased open a few inches. Lucas Atraeus, tall and darkly handsome in evening clothes, was framed in the wash of lamplight.

The small flare of anger that had driven her back to his door leaped a little higher. She had expected Lucas to be somehow diminished in appearance. It didn't help that he still looked heartbreakingly perfect.

The conversation was brief, punctuated by a glimpse of Carla Ambrosi, the woman Lilah realized Lucas truly wanted, hurriedly setting her clothing to rights. In that moment any idea that she could retrieve the situation and persevere with Lucas dissolved.

Gripping the door handle, Lilah wrenched the solid mahogany door closed, cutting Lucas off. In the process the strap of her evening bag flew off her shoulder. Beads scattered as the pretty purse hit the flagstones.

Silence reigned in the corridor for long, nervy seconds. Lilah tried to avoid Zane's gaze. She was so not grieving for the relationship. Somehow she had never managed to get emotionally involved with Lucas. "You knew all along."

He picked up the purse and a number of glittering beads and handed them to her. "They've got a history."

Lilah slipped the little beads into the clutch. "I read the stories two years ago. I guess I should have included the information in my—"

"Wedding planner?"

Her gaze snapped to his. "*Process*. My woman's intuition must have been taking a mini-break."

He lifted a brow. "Don't expect me to apologize for being in touch with my feminine side."

The ridiculous concept of Zane Atraeus possessing any feminine trait broke the tension. "You don't have a feminine side."

A sudden thought blindsided her. Zane in his position as The Atraeus Group's troubleshooter *was* used to handling difficult situations. And employees. "You're running interference for Lucas."

It made perfect sense. With Carla in the mix, Lucas had hedged his bets and asked Zane to fly her out. Now Zane had stepped in to stop her making a scene. It placed her in the realms of being "a problem."

"No."

The flatness of Zane's denial was reassuring. His motives shouldn't matter, but suddenly they very palpably did. She couldn't bear the thought that she was just another embarrassing, or worse, scandalous, situation that Zane was "fixing."

In the distance a door opened. The sharp tap of heels on flagstones, the clatter of dishes, broke the moment.

Zane straightened away from the wall. "You could do with a drink." His hand cupped her elbow. "Somewhere quiet."

The heat of his palm against her bare skin distracted Lilah enough that she allowed him to propel her down the corridor.

Seconds later, Zane opened a door and allowed her to precede him. Lilah stepped into a sitting room decorated in the spare Medinian way, with cream-washed walls, dark furniture and jewel-bright rugs scattered on a flagstone floor. A series of rich oils, no doubt depicting various Atraeus ancestors, decorated the walls. French doors opened out on to one of the many stone terraces that rimmed the castello, affording expansive views of a moonlit Mediterranean sea.

Zane splashed what looked like brandy into a glass. "When did you realize about Lucas and Carla?"

She loosened her death grip on her clutch. "When we arrived at the castello and Carla flung herself into Lucas's arms."

"Then why go to Lucas's room when you had to know what you would find?"

The question, along with the piercing gaze that went with it, was unsettling. She was once again struck by the notion that beneath the urbane exterior Zane was quietly, coldly angry. "I'd had enough of feeling uncomfortable and out of place. Dinner was over and I was tired. I wanted to go back to the hotel."

He pressed the glass into her hands. "With Lucas."

The brush of his fingers sent another zing of awareness through her. "No. Alone."

She sipped brandy and tensed as it burned her throat. She was not about to explain to Zane that she had not gotten as far as thinking about the physical realities of a relationship with his brother. She had assumed all of that would fall into place as they went along. "I put a higher price on myself than that."

"Marriage."

She almost choked on another swallow of brandy. "That's the general idea."

Fingers tightening on the glass, she strolled closer to the paintings, as always drawn by color and composition, the nuances of technique. Jewelry design was her trade, but painting had always been her first love.

She paused beneath an oil of a fierce, medieval warrior, an onyx seal ring on one finger, a scimitar strapped to his back. The straight blade of a nose, tough jaw and magnetic dark gaze were a mirror of Zane's.

Seated beside the warrior was his lady, wearing a parchment silk gown, her exotic gaze square on to the viewer, giving the impression of quiet, steely strength. Lilah was guessing that being married to the brigand beside her, she would need it. An exquisite diamond and emerald ring graced one slim finger; around her neck was a matching pendant.

She felt the heat from Zane's body all down one side as he came to stand beside her. The intangible electrical current that hummed through her whenever he was near grew perceptibly stronger.

Lilah swallowed another mouthful of brandy and tried to ignore the disruptive sensations. The warmth in the pit of her stomach extended to a faint dizziness in her head, reminding her that she had barely eaten at dinner and had already sipped too much wine. She stepped closer to study the jewelry the woman was wearing.

"The Illium jewels."

Lilah frowned, frustrated by the lack of fine detail in the painting. "From Troy? I thought they were a myth."

"They got sold off at the turn of last century when the family went broke. My father managed to buy them back from a private collector."

Lilah noticed the detail of a ship in the background of the painting. "A pirate?"

"A privateer," Zane corrected. "During the eighteen hundreds his seafaring exploits were a major source of wealth for the Atraeus family."

Lilah ignored Zane's smooth explanation. After a brief foray into Medinian history, she had gleaned enough information about the Atraeus family to know that the dark and dangerous ancestor had been a pirate by any other name.

She stepped back from the oil painting in order to appreciate its rich colors. The play of light over the warrior's dark features suddenly made him seem breathtakingly familiar. Exchange the robes, soft boots and a scimitar for a suit and an expensive black shirt and it was Zane. "What was his name?"

"Zander Atraeus, my namesake, near enough. Although my mother didn't have a clue about my father's family history." He turned away. "Finish your drink. I'll take you back to your hotel."

She followed Zane to the sideboard and set her empty brandy glass down. She noticed the glint of the seal ring on the middle finger of Zane's left hand. "Your ring looks identical to the one in the painting."

"It is." His reply was clipped, and she wondered what she had said to cause the cool distance.

Suddenly she understood and busied herself extracting her cell from her clutch. She knew only too well what it was like to be an illegitimate child and excluded from her father's family. As much as she had tried to dismiss that side of the family from her psyche, they still existed and the hurt remained.

"You don't have to take me back to the hotel. I can call a cab." Unfortunately, the screen of her cell was cracked and the phone no longer appeared to work. It must have happened when her purse had gone flying.

Zane checked his watch. "Even if the phone worked, you wouldn't get a cab after midnight on Medinos."

Her stomach sank. She was a city girl; she loved shops, good coffee, public transportation. All the good-natured warnings friends had given her about traveling to a foreign country that was still partway buried in the Middle Ages were coming home to roost. "No underground?"

A flash of amusement lit his dark gaze. "All I can offer is a ride in a Ferrari."

Her stomach tightened on the slew of graphic images that went with climbing into a powerful sports car with Zane Atraeus. It was up there with Persephone accepting a ride from Hades. "Thanks, but no thanks. You don't need to feel responsible for me."

Zane's expression hardened. "Lucas won't be taking you back to the hotel."

Her chin jerked up. "I did get that part." She had been stupidly naive, but not anymore. "Okay, I'll accept the lift to my hotel, but that's all."

Zane's fingers brushed hers as he took her empty glass. "Good. Don't throw yourself away on a man who doesn't value you."

"Don't worry." She stepped back, unnerved by how tempted she was to stay close. "I know exactly how much I'm worth."

She realized how cool and hard that phrase had sounded. "I didn't mean that to sound…like it did."

His expression was neutral. "I'm sure you didn't."

Another memory surfaced. Two weeks after "the kiss," at another function, Zane had found her politely trying to fend off her friend and escort's boss.

She could still remember the hot tingle down her spine, the sudden utter unimportance of the older man who had decided she was desperate to spend the night with him. For an exhilarating moment she had been certain Zane had followed her because he wanted to follow up on the shattering connection she had felt when they had kissed.

Instead, his gaze had flowed through her as if she didn't exist. He had turned on his heel and left.

In a flash of clarity she finally understood why she had agreed to travel to Medinos with a man she barely knew.

The date had been with Lucas, but it was Zane she had always wanted.

In her search for Mr. Dependable she had somehow managed to fixate on his exact opposite.

Lucas had been an unknown quantity and out of her league, but he was nothing compared to Zane. With Zane there would be no guarantees, no safety net, no commitment. The exact opposite of what she had planned for and needed in her life.

Four

Ten days later, Zane stepped into the darkened offices of The Atraeus Group's newest acquisition, Ambrosi Pearls in Sydney. He took the antique elevator, which matched the once-elegant facade of the building, to the top floor.

It was almost midnight; most of the building was plunged into darkness. Zane, who was more used to mining and construction sites and masculine boardrooms, shook his head in bemusement as he strolled into Lucas's office. The air was perfumed; the decor white-on-white. It looked like it had been designed for the editor of a high-end fashion magazine. He noted there was actually a pile of glossy fashion magazines on one end of the curvy designer desk.

Lucas turned from his perusal of downtown Sydney. His hair was ruffled as if he'd run his fingers through it, and his tie was askew. He looked as disgruntled as Zane felt coming off a long flight from Florida.

Zane checked his watch. It was midnight. By his calculations he had been awake almost thirty-six hours. "Why the cloak-and-dagger?"

Lucas stripped off his tie and stuffed the red silk into his pocket. "I've decided to marry Carla. The press is already on the hunt. I've been trying to do a little damage control, but Lilah's going to come under pressure."

Zane's tiredness evaporated. Now the midnight meeting at the office made sense. Lucas's apartment had probably been staked out by the press. "I thought you and Lilah were over."

If he had thought anything else he would not have gone back to Florida to close the land deal. He would have sent someone else.

Lucas paced to the desk, checked the screen of an ice-cream pink cell as if he was waiting for a text, then rifled through a drawer. He came up with a business card. "We are over, but try telling that to the press."

He scribbled a number on the card. "Lilah came to my apartment. She was followed."

Zane took the card. If he thought he had controlled the possessive jealousy that had eaten into him ever since Constantine's wedding, in that moment he knew he was wrong. "What was Lilah doing at your apartment?"

Lucas frowned at the pink cell as if something about it was stressing him to the max. "I'm not sure. Carla was there. Lilah left before I could talk to her. The point is, I need you to mind her for me again."

In terse sentences, Lucas described how a reporter had snapped photos of him kissing Carla out on the sidewalk, with Lilah looking on. The pictures would be published in the morning paper.

Every muscle in Zane's body tensed at the knowledge that Lucas and Lilah were still connected, even if it was only by scandal.

During Constantine's wedding, which Lilah had attended because she had not been able to get a flight out until the following Monday, she had made it clear she was "off" all things Atraeus. Zane had not enjoyed being shut out, but at least he'd had the satisfaction of knowing Lilah was over Lucas.

He wondered what had changed her mind to the extent that she had actually gone to Lucas's apartment. Grimly, he controlled the cavemanlike urge to grab Lucas by his shirtfront, shove him against the wall and demand that he leave Lilah Cole alone. "She won't like it."

Lucas's expression was distracted. "She'll adjust. She's being well compensated."

Zane went still inside. "How, exactly?"

Lucas shuffled papers. "The usual currency. Money, promotion."

Zane could feel his blood pressure rocketing. "Carla won't like that."

"Tell me about it." Lucas shot him a tired grin. "Women. It's a juggling act."

And one in which Lucas, with his killer charm, had always excelled.

Suspicion coalesced into certainty. Despite the engagement to Carla, Zane was certain that Lilah *was* still in the picture for Lucas. Maybe he had it all wrong, but he couldn't allow himself to forget that Lucas had bought Lilah an engagement ring.

He could still see the catalog picture Elena had shown him. The solitaire had been large and flawless. Personally, he had thought the chunky diamond had been a mistake. He would have chosen something antique and lavish, maybe with a few emeralds on the side to match her eyes.

Zane's jaw clenched against the fiery urge to demand to know why, now that Lucas was engaged to Carla, he couldn't leave Lilah Cole alone.

Irrelevant question. Atraeus men had a long, well-publicized history of womanizing. He should know; he was the product of a liaison.

Letting out a breath, Zane forced himself to relax. "How long do you want me to mind her this time?"

Lucas shrugged. "The weekend. Long enough to get her through the media frenzy that's going to break following the announcement at the press conference—" he checked his watch "—today."

Zane's temper frayed at the possessive concern in Lucas's voice. "Sure. We got on okay on Medinos." He drilled Lucas with another cold look. "I think she likes me."

Lucas looked relieved. "Great, I owe you one. I know Lilah isn't your normal type."

Zane's brows jerked together. "What do you mean, not my type?"

Lucas placed his briefcase on the desk and began loading files into it. "Lilah's into classical music; she's arty. I think she paints."

"She does. *I* like art and classical music."

He snapped the case closed. "She's older."

Lucas made the age gap sound like an unbridgeable abyss. "Five years is not a big gap."

Lucas's cell broke into a catchy tango.

Jaw compressed, Zane watched as Lucas snatched up the phone. "Nice tune. Bolero."

Lucas shrugged. "I wouldn't know. This is my secretary's phone. Mine's, uh, broken." He held the cell against his ear and lifted a hand in dismissal. "Hey, thanks."

"Not a problem." Jaw taut, Zane took the creaking elevator to the ground floor. If he had stayed in the office with Lucas much longer he might have lost his temper. He had learned long ago that losing control was the equivalent of losing, and with Lilah Cole he did not intend to lose.

He had to focus, concentrate.

A whole weekend. Two days, *and nights.*

With a woman so committed to marriage she had written a blueprint for success and developed a points system for the men who had scored highly enough to make it into her folder.

Lilah slid dark glasses onto the bridge of her nose and braced herself as she stepped out of her taxi into the midmorning heat of downtown Sydney. Two steps toward the impressive doors of the hotel where the press conference was being held, and a maelstrom of flashing cameras and shouted questions broke over her.

Cheeks hot with embarrassment, she tightened her grip on the ivory handbag that matched her stylish suit, and plowed forward. Someone tugged at the sleeve of her jacket; a flash blinded her. A split second later the grip on her arm and the reporter were miraculously removed, replaced by the burly back of a uniformed security guard. The mass of reporters parted and Zane Atraeus's dark gaze burned into hers, oddly calm and assessing in the midst of chaos. Despite her determination to remain calm in his presence, to forget the kiss, a hot thrill shot down her spine.

"Lilah, come with me."

For a split second she thought he had said, "Lilah, come to me," and the vivid intensity of her reaction to the low, husky command was paralyzing.

She had already had two negative experiences with Atraeus males. Now wasn't the time to redefine that old cliché by fantasizing about jumping out of the frying pan and into the fire, again.

The media surged against the wall of security, an elbow jabbed her back. She clutched Zane's outstretched hand. He released her fingers almost immediately and scooped her against his side, his muscled heat burning into her as they walked.

Three swift steps. The glass doors gleamed ahead. A camera flashed. "Oh, good. More scandal."

She caught the edge of Zane's grin. "That's what you get when you play with an Atraeus."

The hotel doors swished wide. More media were inside, along with curious hotel staff and guests. Lilah worked to keep her expression serene, although she was uncomfortably aware that her cheeks were burning. "I didn't 'play' with anyone."

"You went to Medinos. That was some first date."

The nervy thrill of Zane turning up to protect her evaporated. "I didn't exactly enjoy the experience."

As first dates went it had been an utter disaster.

Zane ushered her into an open elevator. The heat of his palm at the small of her back sent a small shock of awareness through her. Two large Medinian security guards stepped in on either side of them. A third man, blocky and muscled with a shaven head, whom she recognized as Spiros, took up a position by the door and punched buttons.

Lilah's ruffled unease at Zane's closeness increased as the elevator shot upward. "I suppose you're in Sydney for the charity art auction?"

"I'm also doing some work on the Ambrosi takeover, which is why Lucas asked me to mind you."

The last remnants of the intense thrill she had felt when Zane had come looking for her died a death. "I suppose Lucas told you what happened last night?"

"He said you found him with Carla at his apartment."

Lilah's blush deepened. Zane made it sound like she had been involved in some kind of trashy love triangle. "I didn't make it to his apartment. Security—"

"You don't have to explain."

Lilah's gaze narrowed. The surface calm she had been clinging to all morning, ever since she had seen the morning paper, shredded. "Since Medinos, I haven't been able to get an appointment to see Lucas. I got tired of waiting. I was there to resign."

The doors slid open. Adrenaline pumped when she saw the contingent of press in the lobby of the concierge floor, although these weren't the sharp-eyed paparazzi who had been out on the street. She recognized magazine editors, serious tabloids, television news crews.

She took a deep breath as they stepped out of the elevator in the wake of the security team.

Zane's fingers locked around her wrist. "If you run now, what they'll print will be worse."

"Any worse than 'Discarded Atraeus Mistress Abandoned on Street'?"

Zane's expression was grim. "You should have known Lucas was playing out of your league."

Something inside her snapped. "Is it too late to say I wish I'd never met Lucas?"

The moment was freeing. She realized she had never actually connected with Lucas on an emotional level. Marriage with him would have been a disaster.

Zane's gaze captured hers, making her heart pound. "How worried are you about the media?"

Lilah blinked. The focused heat in Zane's eyes was having a mesmerizing effect. "I don't have a TV and I canceled my newspaper subscription this morning. Dealing with the media is not my thing."

"Is this?"

His jaw brushed her forehead. Tendrils of heat shimmered through her at the unexpected contact. His hands framed her face. Dimly, she registered that he intended to kiss her. In the midst of the hum of security, press and hotel staff, time seemed to slow, stop. She was spun back two years to the seductive quiet of the empty reception room, eleven days ago to the flight to Medinos.

She dragged in a shallow breath. She needed to step back, calm down, forget the crazy attraction that zinged through her every time she was near Zane. Constantine and Lucas had both gone through gorgeous women like hot knives through butter, but Zane had a reputation that scorched.

His breath feathered her lips. She closed her eyes and his mouth touched hers, seducingly warm and soft. A shock wave of heat shimmered out from that one small point of contact.

He lifted his head. His gaze, veiled by inky lashes, locked on hers. Instead of straightening, his hands dropped to her waist. The heat from his palms burned through the finely tailored silk as he drew her closer.

The motorized whirr of cameras and the buzz of conversation receded as she clutched at Zane's shoulders and angled her jaw, allowing him more comfortable access. This time the kiss was firmer, heated, deliberate, sizzling all the way to her toes. By the time Zane lifted his mouth, her head was spinning and her legs felt as limp as noodles.

The smattering of applause and wolf whistles shunted her back to earth. She stared at the forest of microphones trying to break through the wall of security, her wild moment of rebellion evaporating.

The phrase "out of the frying pan and into the fire" once more reverberated through her. "Now they'll think I'm sleeping with you as well."

Zane's arm locked around her waist as he propelled her through the reporters and into the room in which the press conference was being held. "Think of it this way, if you're with me, at least now they'll wonder who dumped whom."

Forty-five minutes later the official part of the press conference was over. Lucas and Carla, Lucas's mother, Maria Therese, and Constantine's P.A. Tomas had left in a flurry of publicity over their engagement announcement and the further announcement that Sienna and Constantine were expecting a baby.

Zane flowed smoothly to his feet. "Now we leave."

Relieved that Lucas's announcement had taken the unnerving focus of the press off her, Lilah hooked the strap of her handbag over her shoulder.

Two steps onto the still crowded floor and an elegant blonde backed by a TV crew shoved a mike at Zane. "Can we expect another engagement announcement soon?"

"No comment." Zane lengthened his stride, bypassing the TV crew and the question as he propelled her toward the elevator.

Even though Lilah knew that Zane's lack of response was the only sensible option, his comment left her feeling oddly flat and definitely manipulated.

The end of the nonrelationship with Lucas had not mattered. Standing on the pavement the previous evening while a reporter had snapped her witnessing Lucas and Carla locked in a passionate clinch had not been a feel-good moment. But, as embarrassing as her association with Zane's brother had turned out to be, after the toe-curling intimacy of the kisses in front of the media, in that moment she felt the most betrayed by Zane.

Five

Zane hustled Lilah out into a private underground parking lot and opened the door of a gleaming, low-slung black Corvette. He waited for Lilah to climb into the passenger-side seat then walked around the vehicle and slid behind the wheel.

He had been annoyed enough with Lucas to want to stake a claim on Lilah, although he hadn't planned on doing it in quite such a public way.

He also hadn't expected Lilah to kiss him back quite so enthusiastically. Although ever since they had hit the elevator on the way down she had been cool and reserved and irritatingly distant.

He lifted a hand as Spiros and the two security guards climbed into a black sedan.

He fastened his seat belt. The back of his hand brushed Lilah's. The automatic jolt he received from the brush of her skin against his increased his irritable temper. A temper that, just days ago, he had not known he'd possessed.

The dark sedan the bodyguards had climbed into cruised

out of the parking building. Seconds later, Zane followed, emerging into the glare of daylight.

He transferred his gaze to the woman beside him. Dressed in her signature ivory and white, her hair smoothed into a loose, elegant confection on top of her head, smooth teardrop pearls dangling from tiny lobes, Lilah looked both cool and drop-dead sexy. The fact that he had kissed off her lipstick, leaving her lips bare, only succeeded in making her even more sensually alluring.

Grimly he noted that the same addictive fascination that had tempted him to lose his head two years ago was still at work. Lilah Cole was openly and unashamedly husband-hunting. She was the kind of woman he couldn't afford in his life, and yet it seemed he couldn't resist her.

Lilah stared straight ahead, her purse gripped in her lap. "I know I've been invited to lunch with your family, but with everything that's happened, maybe that isn't such a good idea. If you drop me off, I can get a taxi back to the office."

Zane's jaw tightened at the subdued, worried note in Lilah's voice. Lucas should have known better; he should have left her alone. "It's lunchtime. You need to eat."

She looked out of the passenger window. "I had cereal and toast for breakfast. I'm not exactly hungry."

Zane found the thought of Lilah crunching her way through cereal and toast before facing the press oddly endearing. He wondered what kind of cereal she ate then crushed his curiosity about her.

He braked for a set of lights. "Lucas would probably be relieved if you didn't show."

The words were ruthless, but he had gotten used to seeing Lilah calm and businesslike, with all her ducks in a row. For two years it had been a quality that had irritated him profoundly. Incomprehensibly, he now found himself looking for ways to get her back to her normal, ultraorganized self.

Her gaze snapped to his. "What Lucas wants or does not want is of no concern to me."

Zane felt suddenly happier than he had in days. The lights changed, he put the car in gear and accelerated through the intersection. "I can take you somewhere else to eat if you want."

Her head whipped around, her green gaze shooting fire. "On second thought, no."

"Good. Because we're here."

He watched Lilah study the elegant portico of the Michelin star restaurant as if the fluted columns represented the gates of Hades. "You're a manipulative man."

"I'm an Atraeus."

"Sometimes I forget."

He found himself instantly on the defensive. "Because I'm also a Salvatore?"

He did not voice the other lurking fear that had reared its head since his conversation with Lucas, that it was because he was only twenty-four.

She frowned, as if his shadowy past had not occurred to her. "Because sometimes you're…nice."

"Nice." His brows jerked together.

She looked embarrassed. "I read the article about you on the charity website. I know that you wear those three earrings to help kids relate to you when you do counseling work. You can try all you like to prove otherwise but, from where I come from, that's *nice.*"

Lilah breathed a sigh of relief when Zane pulled in at her apartment's tiny parking area. Lunch had been just as stilted and uncomfortable as she had imagined. Thankfully, the service had been ultraquick and they had been able to leave early.

Zane walked around and opened her door. Lilah climbed out of the low bucket seat, acutely aware of the shadowy cleavage visible in the V of her jacket and of the length of thigh exposed by the shortness of her skirt. When she had dressed that morning, the suit had seemed elegant and circumspect but it was not made for struggling out of a low slung 'Vette.

Zane's gaze locked with hers, making her feel breathless.

She clamped down on the uncharacteristic desire to boldly meet his gaze.

Arriving at the front door of her apartment with a man was what she liked to refer to as a dating "red zone." She and Zane were not dating, but the situation had somehow become more fraught than any dating scenario she had ever experienced. After the kiss earlier, it would not be a good idea to allow Zane inside her house.

She gave him a bright, professional smile. "It's okay, you don't have to see me in. Thanks for the lift."

Zane closed the 'Vette's door and depressed the key lock. "Not a problem. I'll see you to your door."

"That won't be necessary." She aimed another smile somewhere in his general direction as she rummaged in her handbag for her door key.

Zane fell into step beside her. "If I'm not mistaken, that's a reporter staked out over there."

Lilah's head jerked up. She recognized the car that had been parked outside of Lucas's apartment the previous night. Her heart sank. "He must have followed us."

"The car was here when we arrived. According to Lucas, *you* were the one who was followed last night. The press has probably been staking you out ever since you returned from Medinos. In which case, I'd better see you safely inside."

Resigning herself, Lilah walked quickly to the large garage-style door, her cheeks warming as she saw the down-at-heel building through Zane's eyes. A converted warehouse in one of the shabbier suburbs, she had chosen the building because it had been cheerful, arty and spectacularly cheap. The ground floor apartment included a huge light-filled north-facing room that was perfect for painting.

Zane, thankfully, didn't seem to notice how shabby the exterior was, a reminder that he had not spent all of his life in luxurious surroundings.

Unlocking the door, she stepped inside the nondescript foyer, with its concrete floors and cream-washed walls.

Zane slid the door to enclose them in the shadowy space. "How many people live here?"

"A dozen or so." She led the way down a narrow, dim corridor and unlocked her front door. Made of unprepossessing sheet metal, it had once led to some kind of workshop.

She stepped into her large sitting room, conscious of Zane's gaze as he took in white walls, glowing wooden floors and the afternoon sun flooding through a bank of bifold doors at one end.

"Nice." He closed the door and strolled into the center of the room, his gaze assessing the paintings she'd collected from friends and family over the years.

He studied a series of three abstracts propped against one wall. "These are yours."

Her gaze gravitated to the mesmerizingly clean lines of his profile as he studied one of the abstracts. "How do you know that?" She had gotten the paintings ready for sale, but hadn't gotten around to signing them yet.

Faint color rimmed his cheekbones. "I've bought a couple at auction. I also saw your work in a gallery a few weeks back."

A small shock went through her that he had actually bought some of her paintings. "I usually sell most of what I paint through the gallery."

He straightened and peered at a framed photograph of her mother and grandmother. "So money's important."

Her jaw firmed. "Yes."

There was no point in hiding it. Following the recent finance company crashes, her mother's careful life savings had dissolved overnight, leaving her with a mortgage she couldn't pay. Subsisting on a part-time wage, which was all her mother could get in Broome, money had become vital.

Lilah hadn't hesitated. The regular sale of her paintings supplemented her income just enough that she was managing to pay her mother's mortgage as well as cover her rent, but only just.

Her failure to present her resignation to Lucas the previous evening was, in a way, a relief. Resigning from Ambrosi Pearls now would not be a good move for either her or her mother.

A crashing sound jerked her head around. Dropping her bag on the couch, she raced through to her studio in time to glimpse a young man dressed in jeans and a T-shirt, a camera slung over his shoulder, as he clambered out through an open window. A split second later, Zane flowed past her, stepped over a stack of canvases that had been knocked to the floor, and followed the intruder out of the window.

Zane caught the reporter as he hung awkwardly on her back fence. With slick, practiced moves he took the memory stick from the camera and shoved what was clearly an expensive piece of equipment back at the reporter's chest.

The now white-faced reporter scrambled over the fence and disappeared into the sports field on the other side.

While Zane examined the fence and walked the boundary of her tiny back garden, Lilah hurriedly tidied up the collapsed pile of canvases.

Her worst fears were confirmed when she discovered a portrait of Zane she had painted almost two years ago, after the disastrous episode on the couch. Zane had practically stepped over the oil to get out of the window. It was a miracle he hadn't noticed.

Gathering the canvases, she stacked them against the nearest wall, so only the backs were visible. She'd had a lucky escape. The last thing she needed now was for Zane to find out that she had harbored a quiet, unhealthy little obsession about him for the past two years.

Zane climbed back in the window and examined the broken catch. "That's it, you're not staying here tonight. You're coming with me. If that reporter made it into your back garden, others will."

Lilah's response was unequivocal. Given that Zane seemed to bring out her wild Cole side, going with him was a very bad idea.

Her cheeks burned as he stared at the backs of the paintings. "That won't be necessary. I'll get the window repaired. I've got a friend in the building who's handy with tools."

She led the way out of the room, away from the incriminating paintings.

His expression grim, Zane checked the locks on the windows of her main living room. "Your studio window is the least of your problems. You've got a sports field next door. That means plenty of off-road parking and unlimited access. Even with a security detail keeping watch front and back, the press won't have any problems getting pictures through all this glass."

"I can draw the curtains. They can't take pictures if there's nothing to see."

"You'll get harassed every time you walk outside or leave the house, and that fence is a major problem. Put it this way, if you don't come with me now, I'm staying here with you." He studied her plain black leather couch as if he was eyeing it up for size.

Lilah's stomach flip-flopped as images of that other couch flashed through her mind. There was no way she could have Zane staying the night in her home. The kissing had been unsettling enough. The last thing she needed was for him to invade her personal space, sleep on *her* couch. "You can't stay here."

Her phone rang and automatically went to the answering machine. The message was audible. A reporter wanted her to call him.

Lilah's gaze zeroed in on the number of messages she had waiting: twenty-three. She didn't think the machine held that many. "I'll pack."

Six

Minutes later, Lilah was packed. Zane, who had spent the time talking into a cell phone, mostly in Medinian, the low, sexy murmur of his voice distracting, snapped the phone closed and slipped it into his pants pocket. "Ready?"

The easy transition from Medinian to American-accented English was startling, pointing out to Lilah, just in case she had forgotten, that Zane Atraeus was elusive *and* complicated. Every time she tried to pigeonhole him as an arrogant, self-centered tycoon, he pushed her off balance by being unexpectedly normal and nice.

While he took her suitcase, Lilah double-checked the locks. On impulse, she grabbed one of her design sketchpads then stepped out into the sterile hall, closing the heavy door behind her.

Zane was waiting, arms folded over his chest, a look of calm patience on his face.

"I'll just leave a message for a neighbor and see if he'll fix the window."

Taking a piece of paper out of her purse, she penned a quick note. Walking a few steps along the dingy corridor, she knocked, just in case Evan was home. She didn't expect him to be in until later in the day, so she slipped the note under his door. The door swung open as she turned to walk away. Evan, looking paint-stained and rumpled, stood there, the note in his hands.

"I didn't think you'd be here until tonight."

Evan was a high-end accountant and painter, and was also a closet gay. The apartment was something in the way of a retreat for him. She had been certain he would stay clear until the press lost interest.

Evan stared pointedly past her at Zane. "It's my day off. I thought I'd come over early just in case you needed a shoulder."

"She doesn't," Zane said calmly.

Evan's expression was suspiciously blank, which meant he was speculating wildly. "Not a problem." He transferred his gaze to Lilah. "Don't worry, I'll fix the window. Call me if you need *anything* else."

Zane held the front door of the apartment building for her. "So, you're still seeing Peters."

Lilah shielded her gaze from the sun as she stepped outside. "How do you know Evan's name?"

Zane loaded her case into the limited rear space of the Corvette. "Peters has a certain reputation with commercial law. So does his boss, Mark Britten."

She could feel her automatic blush at the mention of Evan's boss, the man who had been convinced she was dying to sleep with him before Zane's appearance had ended the small, embarrassing scuffle.

She descended as gracefully as she could into the Vette's passenger seat. "Evan is a *friend*." It was on the tip of her tongue to tell Zane that Evan was gay, but that would mean breaking a confidence. "He paints in his spare time. He doesn't live here. This is just where he keeps his studio."

When they pulled away from the curb, Lilah noticed that Zane's security pulled in close behind them. The ominous black sedan, filled with blocky, muscular men—the leading henchman, Spiros, behind the wheel—looked like something off a movie set. A cream van splashed with colorful graphics idled out of the shadows and slotted in behind the sedan.

Zane glanced in the rearview mirror and made a call on his cell. When he slipped the phone back in his pocket, he glanced at her. "The van's a press vehicle."

"And Spiros is taking care of it?"

Zane's gaze was enigmatic, reminding her of the gulf that existed between his life and hers. "That's what he's paid to do."

Zane inserted the key card in the door of his hotel suite and allowed Lilah to precede him into the room.

Unlocking his jaw he finally addressed the topic that had obsessed him from the moment he had recognized Evan Peters and realized that not only were he and Lilah "friends" of long standing, they were practically living together. "How long have you known Peters?"

There was a moment of silence while she surveyed the heavy opulence of the suite. "Six years. Maybe seven. We met at a painting class."

"When did he move in next door?"

His question was somewhat lost as Lilah strolled through the overstuffed room. The suite, he realized, with its curvy furniture, swagged silk drapes and gilt embellishment might not suit him, but it was a perfect setting for Lilah. Even dressed in the modern suit, she looked lush and exotic, like the expensive courtesans that, before Medinos had become a Christian nation, had been kept closeted in luxury behind lacy wrought iron grills.

She trailed one slim hand over the back of a brocade couch. "As a matter of fact, I was the one who moved next door to him. Evan knew I was looking for a bigger place. When the apartment became available he let me know. It was ideal for what I wanted, so I snapped it up."

His jaw tightened. "And it was a bonus living so close to Peters."

Lilah dropped her purse on the couch and paused to examine an ornate oval mirror. She met his gaze in the glass. "Evan and I are not involved. As you put it, he has a certain reputation in the business world. His painting and some of his artistic friends don't fit the profile, so he keeps that part of his life under wraps."

Involvement or not, it was the knowledge that Peters had likely shared Lilah's bed that bothered him.

Although it had not been the blond accountant's portrait lying on the floor in Lilah's studio. Or Mark Britten's, or Lucas's.

The portrait had been his.

Before he could probe further, his new P.A., Elena, who occupied a single room down the corridor, appeared. Plump but efficiently elegant in a dark suit and trendy pink spectacles, Elena had a clipboard in hand. Spiros appeared in Elena's wake and carried Lilah's bag through to the spare bedroom.

Zane made brief introductions and signed the correspondence on Elena's clipboard. He suppressed his irritation at Elena's bright-eyed perusal of Lilah and the fascinated glances she kept directing his way. No doubt she had read some of the more lurid stories printed about him, which would explain why she seemed to think he needed chocolate-dipped strawberries and oysters on the half shell in his fridge. If she knew how he had lived over the past two years, he thought grimly, she would not have bothered.

When both Elena and Spiros were gone, Zane shrugged out of his jacket, tossed it over a nearby chair and strolled to the doorway of Lilah's room.

The pressing questions surrounding the portrait she had painted of him were replaced by a sense of satisfaction as he watched her unload clothing into a huge, ornate dresser. In *his* suite.

Maybe his personal assistant wasn't so far off in her opinion of him.

According to the history books, on his various raids, Zander Atraeus hadn't confined himself to stealing jewels. At that moment, he formed a grim insight into how his marauding ancestor must have felt when he had stolen away the woman he had eventually married.

Lilah glanced up, a stylish jewelry case in one hand. "Your P.A. doesn't approve."

He settled his shoulder against the door frame, curiously riveted by the feminine items she placed with calm precision on top of the dresser. "Elena had a traditional Medinian upbringing. She would probably prefer you in a separate suite for propriety's sake."

Her expression brightened. "Great idea."

"You're staying here, where I can keep an eye on you. All the suites and rooms at this end of the corridor are booked out to Atraeus staff. It's safe because no one comes in or out without security checking."

"What about the publicity?"

He shrugged. "Whether you have a separate room or share this suite, after what happened this morning, the story they print will be the same. This way, at least, *I* know where you are."

She zipped her empty case closed and placed it in the closet. "What I can't figure out is why that should be so important to you."

"I made a promise to Lucas."

Hurt registered briefly in her gaze. "Silly me," she muttered breezily. "I forgot." Pushing open the terrace door, she stepped out onto the patio.

Zane caught her before she had gone more than a few feet. "Not a good idea. The terrace isn't safe."

On the heels of the hurt that Zane was only following Lucas's orders in looking after her, Zane's grip on her arm sent a small shock of adrenaline plunging through her veins.

She took a panicked half step, at the same time twisting to free herself. In the process her heel skidded on the paver. A sharp little pain signaled that she had managed to turn her ankle.

"What is it?"

She balanced on one heel. "It's not serious." It was the shoe that was the problem; there was something not quite right with the heel.

A split second later she found herself lifted up, carried back inside and deposited on the bed.

Zane removed the offending shoe, which had a broken heel, tossed it on the floor then examined her ankle. The light brush of his fingers sent small shivers through her. "Stay there. I'll get some ice."

"There's no need, honestly."

But he had already gone.

Wiggling her foot, which felt just fine, Lilah stared at the ornately molded ceiling, abruptly speechless. Gold cherubs encircled a crystal chandelier, which she hadn't previously noticed.

She pushed up into a reclining position, and eased back into the decadent luxury of a satin quilted headboard and a plump nest of down pillows. She wiggled her ankle. There was barely a twinge, nothing she couldn't walk off.

Before she could slide off the bed, Zane appeared with a plastic bag filled with ice cubes. The enormous bed depressed as he sat down and placed the ice around her ankle.

She winced at the cold and tried not to love the fact that he was looking after her. "It's really not that bad."

He placed a cushion under her ankle to elevate it. "This way it won't get bad. Just stay put."

He rose to his feet, his expression taking on a look of blunt possession that was oddly thrilling, and that soothed the moment of hurt when she had thought he viewed her as a problem. She decided that in the rich turquoise-and-gold decadence of the room, and despite his kindness over her ankle, she had no trouble placing Zane at all.

When someone looked like a pirate and acted like a pirate, they very probably were a pirate.

An hour on the bed without anything to read and no chance of drowsing off because she was on edge at being in Zane's suite, and Lilah had had enough.

Pushing into a sitting position, she swung her legs over the edge of the bed. She put weight on the foot. A few steps, with the barest of twinges, and she judged it was perfectly sound. The ice pack, which she had taken into her bathroom as soon as Zane had left the room, was melting in the bathtub.

She checked the sitting room, relieved to see that it was empty, and noted the sound of water running, indicating that Zane was having a shower. After changing into jeans and a white camisole, she brushed her hair and wound it back into a tidy knot. Collecting her sketchpad and a pencil, she slipped dark glasses on the bridge of her nose and stepped out onto the terrace. A recliner was placed directly outside her room.

Flipping the pad open, to her horror she discovered that she had picked up the wrong pad. Instead of her latest jewelry sketches, ornate pearl items based on a set of traditional Medinian pieces, she found herself staring at a charcoal sketch of intent dark eyes beneath straight brows, mouthwatering cheekbones and a strong jaw.

Flipping through the book, she studied page after page of sketches, which she had done over a two-year period. Slamming the book closed, she stared at the blank office buildings and hotels across the street. Until that moment she hadn't realized how fixated she had become.

She had simply drawn Zane when she had felt the urge. The problem was the urge had become unacceptably frequent. It was no wonder that in the past two years she'd had trouble whipping up any enthusiasm for her dates. She had even begun to worry about her age; after all she was nearly thirty.

She had even considered dietary supplements, but clearly food wasn't the problem.

A shadow falling over the sketchpad shocked her out of her reverie.

Zane, wearing black jeans that hung low on narrow hips, his muscled chest bare. "You shouldn't be out here. I told you, it isn't safe."

Lilah dragged her gaze from the expanse of muscled flesh, the intriguing tracery of scars on his abdomen. She was abruptly glad for the screen her dark glasses provided. "We're twenty stories up, with security controlling access to this part of the hotel. I don't see how this terrace can not be safe."

"For the same reason I have bodyguards. The Atraeus family has a lot of money. That attracts some wacky types."

"Is that how you got the scars?"

He leaned down and braced his hands on the armrests on either side of the recliner, suddenly suffocatingly close. "I got the scars when I was a kid, because I didn't have either money or protection. Since my father picked me up, no one's gotten that close, mostly because I listen to what my chief of security tells me."

She stared at his freshly shaven jaw, trying to ignore the scents of soap and cologne. "Which is?"

"That no matter how sunny the day looks, there are a lot of bad people out there, so you don't take risks and you do what you're told." He lifted her dark glasses off the bridge of her nose.

She released her grip on the sketchpad to reclaim the sunglasses. Zane let her have the glasses, but straightened, taking her sketchpad with him.

Irritation at the sneaky trick, followed by mortification that he might glance through and discover her guilty secret, burned through her. "Give that back."

She caught the edge of his grin as he stepped into the shadowy interior of the sitting room. Launching off the recliner, she raced after him, blinking as she adjusted to the dimness of the sitting room. She made a lunge for the pad. Zane evaded her reach by taking a half step back.

"Why do you need it so badly?" His gaze was curiously intent, making her stomach sink.

"Those sketches are…private."

And guiltily, embarrassingly revealing.

The drawings cataloged just how empty her private life had been. He would know just how much she had thought about him, focused on him and how often.

He handed her the pad but instead of letting it go, used it to draw her closer by degrees until her knuckles brushed the warm, hard muscles of his chest.

The relief that had spiraled through her when she thought he hadn't checked out the drawings dissolved. "You *looked*."

"Uh-huh." Gaze locked with hers, he drew her close enough that her thighs brushed his and the sketchpad, which she was clutching like a shield, was flattened between them.

He lifted a dark brow. "And you would be drawing and painting me because…?"

Lilah briefly closed her eyes. The old cliché about wishing the ground would open up and swallow her had nothing on this. "You saw the painting in my apartment."

"It was hard to miss."

She drew in a stifled breath. "I was hoping you wouldn't."

"Because then you could avoid admitting that you're attracted to me. And have been ever since we met two years ago."

Gently, he eased the sketchpad from her grip. "You don't need that anymore." He tossed the pad aside. "Not when you have the real thing."

Seven

Lilah was frozen to the spot, gripped by the inescapable knowledge that if she wanted Zane, he wanted her. "Maybe I prefer the fantasy."

"Liar." His head dipped, his forehead touched hers. "What now?" The question was soft and flat.

"Nothing." She swallowed, unable to take her gaze from his mouth, or to forget the memory of the kisses that morning.

Just that morning. In the interim a lot had happened. The passage of time seemed wildly distorted, as if days had passed, not hours.

And that was when she understood what had happened.

Somehow she had done the very thing she had worked to avoid. She had allowed herself to get caught in the grip of a physical obsession. And not just any obsession.

She stared into the riveting depths of Zane's eyes. She had followed a path well-trodden by Cole women. She had fallen victim to the *coup de foudre*.

That was why she had ended up on the couch with Zane.

It explained her inability to say "no" to kissing Zane on the flight and during the press conference.

Somehow, without her quite knowing how, she had allowed sex to sabotage her life.

Zane's gaze narrowed. "Don't look at me like that."

"Like what?" But she knew.

Her guilty secret had been exposed, the emotions and longings she had kept quietly tucked away—all the better to deny them—had been forced to the surface.

And Zane wasn't helping the process. Instead of backing off, he was making no bones about the fact that he liked it that she wanted him.

He dipped his head to kiss her. Lifting up on her toes, she wound her arms around his neck and met him halfway.

It was crazy. She hardly knew him, but already she knew how to fit herself against him, how to angle her jaw so his mouth could settle against hers.

With a stifled groan, he wrapped her close. Half lifting her, he walked her backward across the sitting room. Somewhere in the distance, Lilah registered the phone ringing, then they were in his room. The back of her knees hit the edge of his bed.

He came down beside her. Conscious thought evaporated as his mouth reclaimed hers. Long minutes later, he rolled and pulled her on top of him, his fingers tangling in her hair. Charmed and utterly seduced by the clear invitation to play, to kiss him back, she framed his face and lowered her mouth to his.

His palms smoothed down the curve of her spine, pressing her against him so that she was intimately aware of every curve and plane of heated muscle, the firm shape of his arousal. On the upward journey, he peeled her camisole up until he met the barrier of her bra.

Murmuring something short and soft beneath his breath, he fumbled at the fastening then shifted his hands around to cup her breasts.

The distinctive sound of the front door opening cut through

the dizzying haze. Elena, dressed in a shimmering, ankle-length black dress and looking like a sleek well-fed raven in spectacles, appeared in the doorway to Zane's room.

Zane muttered something short beneath his breath and rolled over in an attempt to shield Lilah from his assistant's view.

Cheeks flushed, Lilah dragged her camisole back into place.

Elena dragged her fascinated gaze from Zane's chest and seemed to remember herself. She checked the dainty watch on her wrist and addressed Zane in rapid Medinian.

Zane rose to his feet and pulled on a shirt that was draped over a nearby chair. "English, please, Elena."

"The car is ready. Gemma, your, uh, *date*—" she directed an apologetic glance at Lilah "—is waiting. Providing we reach the museum in the next twenty minutes, we won't be late."

Gemma. Lilah jackknifed. She was Zane's previous personal assistant and the pretty redhead he had escorted to almost every function the charity had held over the last two years.

Hurt shimmered through her. Above all the gorgeous girls Zane had dated, Gemma reigned supreme. Zane always went back to her. If Lilah had been tempted to fantasize about any kind of a future with Zane, this was exactly the wake-up call she needed.

A second salient fact registered. The museum. And an auction of a private art collection that had been donated to the charity.

Somehow in the craziness of the past few days, she had forgotten she was supposed to attend. Frantically, she checked her wristwatch.

She should have been dressed by now and calling a taxi.

Another thought occurred to her. "Howard."

Zane's head snapped around as he shrugged into a shirt. He gave her a questioning look.

"My date." She scrambled off the bed. She was supposed to be meeting Howard outside the museum in fifteen minutes.

She dashed into her room, snatched an uncrushable cream dress off its hanger, dressed and fixed her hair. She slipped into cream heels and applied a quick dash of mascara and lip-gloss, a spray of her favorite perfume and she was ready.

Picking up her clutch, she joined Zane and Elena. The venue wasn't far away, but there was no way she would make her rendezvous with Howard in time. To compound matters, this was a first date recommended by the online dating agency she had started using just weeks ago. She had never physically met Howard. All she knew was that he had ticked all the boxes in terms of her requirements in a husband.

Now that Lucas was history, Howard was number one on her list of eligible bachelors and her most likely prospect for marriage.

She dragged her gaze from the riveting sight of Zane in a black tuxedo, and tried to gloss over the fact that she had just climbed out of his bed and was now going to meet a prospective husband. "I need a lift to the museum."

Lilah was five minutes late.

Howard White was waiting in the appointed place in the museum foyer, although at first she had difficulty picking him out because he was older than the photograph he had supplied. Mid-forties, she guessed, rather than the age of thirty-two, which he had given.

Flustered and ashamed at herself for her loss of control with Zane, and for forgetting she was even meeting Howard, Lilah resolved to overlook his dishonesty.

Howard smiled pleasantly as they shook hands. "I feel like I know you already."

Guilt burned through her as Howard continued to study her in a way that was just a little too familiar for comfort.

Her picture *had* been splashed across the tabloids. Her only hope now was that he wouldn't put two and two together when he saw Zane. She would have to do her best to make sure that they were not seen together.

As he released her hand, she couldn't help but notice that he had a pale strip across the third finger of his left hand, which seemed to indicate that Howard had been recently married.

The evening progressed at a snail's pace.

Burningly aware of Zane just a short distance away with Gemma clinging on his arm, Lilah found it hard to focus on Howard and his accounting business.

Howard placed his empty mineral water on a nearby side table and beckoned a passing waiter. "Are you sure you wouldn't like some champagne?"

"No. Thank you." Lilah was beginning to get a little annoyed at the pressure Howard was applying with regard to alcohol, especially when he had not touched anything alcoholic himself.

"Very sensible." He put his wallet away.

She tried to think of something else to say, but the conversation had staggered to a halt.

Howard jerked at his collar as if it was too tight. "My—uh, mother doesn't agree with alcohol, especially not for women."

Lilah dragged her gaze from Zane's profile. She had barely paid Howard any attention, but all of her Cole instincts were on high alert. She had received the strong impression that Howard had been about to say "wife." "Your *mother?*"

Howard's gaze shifted to the auctioneer, who was just setting up. He dragged at his tie as if he was having trouble breathing. "I live with my, uh, mother. She's a fine woman."

Feeling suddenly wary of Howard, Lilah excused herself on the grounds that she needed some fresh air before the auction started.

She stepped outside onto a small paved terrace dotted with modern sculpture. A footfall sounded behind her. Zane. Light slanted across his cheekbones, making him look even tougher and edgier.

She had been aware that he had been keeping an eye on her the entire time and had hoped he would follow her.

He jerked his head in the direction of the crowded room. "When did you meet him?"

"Tonight."

His expression was incredulous. "A blind date?"

She stared at the soaring, shadowy shape of a concrete obelisk, as if the outline was riveting. "More or less."

It was none of Zane's business that Howard had contacted her through her online dating service. His application was very recent. It had appeared in her in-box just before she had gone to Medinos. She had felt raw enough on her return that she had agreed to her first actual date.

"I don't like him, and you're not leaving with him." There was a vibrating pause. "He's old enough to be your father."

There was an oddly accusing note to Zane's voice. Lilah stared hard at a tortured arrangement of pipes at the center of the small courtyard, a piece of art that, according to a plaque, had something to do with the inner-city "vibe." "He is older than I thought."

She rubbed her bare arms against the coolness of the night, suddenly desperate to change the subject. "Where's Gemma?"

"Gemma won't miss me for a few minutes. Is that why you dated Lucas, because he was older?"

Her gaze connected with Zane's. She didn't know why he was so stuck on the issue of age. "I don't see what this has to do with anything."

"I've read your personnel file. I know how old you are, I also know that you seem to date older men. Is that a requirement for your future husband?"

Despite the chilly air it was suddenly way too hot. She tried to whip up some outrage that Zane had accessed her personal information, but the implications of his prying were riveting. She couldn't think of any reason for Zane to focus on the age of her dates unless it affected him personally. The thought that

Zane was comparing himself with her dates and that he was actually worried that he was too young, was dizzying. "No."

Something like relief flickered in his gaze. "Good."

His fingers linked with hers, drew her close.

Lilah swallowed against the sudden dryness in her mouth. After the disaster on Medinos followed by the deadening effect of Howard's company, Zane's interest in her was fatally seductive. "This is a bad idea. You're with someone else."

In theory so was she, but Howard, with his sneaky lies and deceptions, had ceased to count.

"Gemma works for The Atraeus Group. She just helps me out on occasion."

Zane's head dipped, his breath wafted over her cheek, and suddenly, irresistibly, they were back where they'd been less than two hours ago—on the verge of...something.

His lips touched hers. Heat shivered through her, she lifted up on her toes. Her palms automatically slid over his shoulders, fingers digging into pliant muscle. His hands closed on her waist.

The sound of the auctioneer taking bids flowed out into the night, but even that faded as she stepped closer, angled her chin and leaned into the kiss.

Something shifted in the shadows, flashed. Zane's head jerked up.

A second shadow flickered. A night security officer with a flashlight in one hand nodded as he walked past.

Confused, Lilah stepped back from Zane. For a moment she was certain someone had used a camera flash. She couldn't stop the gossip and the sensationalized stories, but that didn't mean she had to like the sneakiness of the reporters. "I'd better go back inside. Howard will be missing me."

Zane was still watching the shadowy figure of the security officer as he stepped into a concealed side entrance. "Are you serious about him?"

"Not anymore." Feeling a wrenching regret at leaving the courtyard, Lilah made her way back into the crowded room.

Howard was still engrossed in conversation with a knot of older men. He didn't bother to look her way. Lilah decided that Zane was right; he looked depressingly paternal.

Zane fell into step beside her. His fingers closed on hers.

Pleasure and guilty heat shooting through her, Lilah jerked her fingers free. Zane's teasing grin made her heart pound. She resisted the almost overpowering urge to smile back. "What do you think you're doing?"

The wicked grin faded. "Something I should have done before, checking out your date. I want to make sure Howard doesn't have an agenda."

"He does. I realized tonight that he's married."

Zane's expression went from irritated to remote as he slid his cell out of his pocket and spoke briefly into it.

He snapped the phone closed. "Go to the car with Gemma and Elena. Spiros has just pulled up to the curb outside. I'll deal with Howard. Your boyfriend was also out in the court-yard with a phone camera."

Lilah stared at Howard who she noticed, was now knocking back something that looked extremely alcoholic. She remembered the shuffling sound, the extra flash.

Zane inserted himself into the jovial male group with the confidence and ease that came from being a supreme preda-tor in the business world. She saw the moment Howard real-ized he had been made, the automatic reach for his pocket as if he wanted to shield his cell phone.

Howard's wild gaze connected briefly with hers. With calm deliberation, Lilah turned her back on Howard and walked through to the museum lobby. She noted that she didn't feel in the least shocked or depressed by the betrayal. On the con-trary, there had been something highly satisfying in watch-ing Zane go into battle for her. Unfortunately, along with her new ruthless streak, she seemed to have also gotten used to leading a life of notoriety.

Gemma and Elena strolled out directly behind her. Spiros held the door for them while they climbed into the limousine.

Elena chatted with Spiros in Medinian, leaving Lilah with a clearly unhappy Gemma.

Seconds later Zane joined them. Gemma beamed and patted the vacant space beside her. Instead of climbing in, Zane glanced across at a group of boys Lilah had noticed loitering a small distance away from the limo.

He glanced at Lilah. "I won't be long."

Gemma, looking distinctly irritable as Zane walked over to the boys, extracted a cell from her clutch and within seconds was deep in conversation about her new job and a move overseas. Elena retrieved a romance novel from her clutch, attached an efficient looking little LED light to the back pages, and was promptly engrossed.

Lilah decided she clearly hadn't lived, because she hadn't thought to bring an activity with her that was suitable for downtime in a limousine. Absently, she noted Howard slinking off to his car, which turned out to be a sleek little hatchback with a personalized licence plate that read "HERS."

Zane terminated a cell phone conversation as he walked back to the car. "I can't come back to the hotel with you right now. I have to take care of these kids. They saw the posters for the charity auction—that's why they came."

Lilah stared across at the lean wraiths clustered around a park bench as if that small landmark was all they had. "What can you do?"

"Get them in a house for the night with state foster care. That doesn't guarantee they'll stay, but at least it's a start. I'll see you later."

Lilah watched as Zane walked back to the kids, seeing the instant brightening of their faces. She hadn't realized how personally involved he was, or how much kids liked him.

She felt like she was seeing him for the first time, not the quintessential bad boy or the exciting, elusive lover the media liked to publicize, but a committed, protective man who would make an excellent father.

With the rest of the night in Zane's hotel suite looming,

it was not a good time to discover that Zane had somehow managed to transcend the list of attributes she was searching for in a husband and had made her requirements seem petty and flawed.

Eight

Lilah's cell phone rang as she stepped in the door of the suite. It was Zane. She remembered that she had given him her number earlier.

"Stay in my room. I won't be late."

She stiffened at the invitation, as if Zane was already so sure of her he assumed she would be sleeping with him. "No."

There was a hollow pause. "Why not?"

"For a start, you already have a girlfriend."

"Gemma is not my girlfriend. Like I said, she's a company employee and she fills in as my escort on occasion. Tonight's date was organized a few weeks ago. I would have canceled if I'd had time."

Lilah's fingers tightened on the phone. "I know this might sound silly to you, but I made a certain…vow. I might have forgotten it for a few minutes this afternoon, but that doesn't change the fact that it's important to me."

There was a ringing silence, punctuated by raised voices in the background.

"I have to go," Zane said curtly. "Whatever you do, don't leave the suite. Spiros will be out in the corridor if you need anything. And don't use the hotel phone. It's not secure and the press are still camped in the foyer."

The phone clicked quietly in her ear.

Feeling suddenly flat and a little depressed, Lilah walked through to her room and showered in the opulent marble bathroom, which not only contained a large walk-in shower, but a sunken spa tub. After slipping on a silk chemise, she belted one of the fluffy hotel robes around her waist and walked back out to the kitchen.

She found a bowl of fruit and a basket of fresh rolls on the counter. The fridge was groaning with food.

Abruptly starving, because she had been too wound up to eat anything but a few canapés from the buffet at the auction, Lilah helped herself to bread and cheese and a selection of mouthwatering dishes from the fridge. To balance out the decadence, she made herself a cup of tea.

Loading her snack onto a small tray, she carried it through to the sitting room and set it down on an elegant coffee table. She flicked through TV channels until she found a local news station.

Wrong choice. She stared at the live footage of Zane with Gemma at some point during the charity auction that evening. Her arm was coiled snugly around his. Young and fresh, with an ultrasexy fuchsia gown, Gemma was the perfect foil for Zane's dark, powerful build.

Suddenly miserable, she flicked to another channel and stared blankly at an old black-and-white movie. At eleven o'clock, she turned the TV set off. Too restless to sleep and worried that her apartment might have been broken into, she decided to call Evan and check if he had managed to fix the window. She retrieved her cell from her handbag and discovered the battery was dead. In her hurry to pack, she had not included her cell phone charger.

She spent another half hour kicking her heels. Her irritation at her isolation in the fabulous suite was edged by the dreaded notion that maybe Zane hadn't yet returned because he was now with Gemma.

It wasn't as if she had a claim on Zane, or should want to make one. Despite the attraction that sizzled between them, the crazy, inappropriate sense of attachment, Zane Atraeus did not fit into her life.

The one area in which they were in complete harmony was the most dangerous part of their relationship. No matter how tempted she was to fall into bed with Zane, she couldn't forget that sex had gotten her mother and her grandmother into trouble, literally.

At eleven-thirty, she retreated to her bedroom, climbed into the Hollywood fantasy of a bed and tried to sleep.

At midnight, tired of tossing and turning in a tangle of silken bedclothes, she pushed out of bed and walked back out to the kitchenette. On impulse, she picked up the hotel directory, found out how to dial out and called Evan, who was a night owl and didn't normally go to bed until one or two o'clock.

Evan was terse and to-the-point. He *had* fixed the window, but now he was busy, entertaining a *friend*.

Cheeks burning, Lilah apologized. She was on the point of hanging up when Zane walked through the door.

Zane shrugged out of his jacket and tossed it over the back of a chair. "I thought I told you not to use the hotel phone."

Lilah said goodbye and hung up. "I had to make a call. My cell phone battery was dead."

He frowned. "Who is it? Howard?"

"No."

"Lucas?"

"I called Evan to see if he'd fixed my window."

He removed his bow tie and jerked at the buttons of his dress shirt. "Peters. Just how many male friends have you got?"

Annoyance zinged through her. "I don't know why that

should worry you, when you've got so many 'friends' yourself."

Zane's expression cleared, as if she had just said something that had cheered him up immeasurably. "I've spent half the night with a bunch of scared kids."

She stared resolutely at his jaw, desperate to avoid the softening in his gaze. "It's after midnight."

Comprehension gleamed. "And you thought I was with Gemma."

He closed the distance between them and framed her face so she was forced to meet his gaze, and suddenly there was no air. "Why do you think I became the patron of a Sydney charity, when I've been based in the States?"

Zane answered his own question. "Because I wanted you."

Zane logged the moment Lilah accepted that he genuinely wanted her.

Desire burned away the jealousy that had gripped him when he had found her talking on the phone.

He didn't *get* jealous. Ever since his early teens, he had controlled his emotions and his sex drive. He had been selective in his bed partners.

For two years, since he had severed his last short liaison, he hadn't needed a woman at all. It was not unusual for him to have periods of celibacy, but this one had stretched beyond personal preference.

Lilah's sea-green gaze locked with his.

The attraction didn't make sense. He didn't want Lilah to matter to him, but it was a fact that she did.

Bending his head, he touched his mouth to hers.

Long, drugging seconds passed. He lifted his head before he lost it completely. He was male, he loved women, their softness and beauty; he just didn't trust them.

Until now, he'd had no interest in changing.

The thought that he could change, that he wanted to trust Lilah, made his heart pound.

Her fingers slid into his hair. The faint, tugging pressure

as she lifted up and pressed her mouth to his was stunningly erotic. A wave of intense, dissolving pleasure shimmered through him. Dimly, he noted that he was on the edge of losing control.

Lilah lifted up on her toes, pressing closer to Zane. Subconsciously, she realized she had been waiting for this ever since Elena had interrupted them that afternoon.

With a stifled groan, Zane took a half step forward, pinning her against the edge of the counter.

She felt him tugging at her thick, fluffy robe, the coolness of the air against her skin as the robe slipped to the floor. He dipped his head and took one breast in his mouth through the silk of her chemise, and sensation jerked through her.

A split second later, the room tilted as he swung her into his arms. Depositing her on the soft cushions of one of the elaborate, overstuffed couches, he came down alongside her.

Blindly, she fumbled at his shirt until she found naked skin. She tore open the final buttons and impatiently waited while he shrugged out of the shirt.

She felt the heat of his palms gliding along her thighs, the warm silk of her chemise puddling around her hips.

In twelve years of dating, this was the closest she had come to feeling anything like the intensity that friends wept over and talked about, that she had absorbed second hand through books and movies.

Being desired, she discovered, was infinitely seductive; it undermined her defenses, dissolved every last shred of resistance. Even the idea of holding on to her virginity seemed vague and abstract. Especially in light of the fact that she had already more or less surrendered to Zane two years ago. After grimly hanging on to that bastion of purity for so long she couldn't help thinking it might actually be a relief to get rid of it.

Zane's fingers hooked in the waistband of her panties. Driven by desire and an intense curiosity, instead of resisting, Lilah lifted her hips and assisted the process. Cool air was instantly replaced by the muscular heat of Zane's body as he came down between her legs.

As wrong as her logical mind told her it was to allow Zane to make love to her, the man who was holding her, cradling her as if she was precious to him, *felt* right. She had never felt more alive; she couldn't help adoring every minute. In that moment she understood why both her mother and grandmother had risked all for passion. She couldn't believe she had waited this long to find out.

In an effort to help out, she tugged at the fastening of his pants, and felt him hot and silky smooth against her. His heated gaze locked with hers. For a moment, time seemed to stand still. Then he surged inside her.

Zane froze.

His gaze locked with Lilah's again. Comprehension sliced through the spiraling pleasure that for the past few minutes had numbed his brain. "You're a virgin."

Her expression was distracted, although she didn't seem overly upset. "Yes."

He wasn't wearing a condom. That was another first.

Zane's jaw clenched as wave after wave of raw desire washed through him. He had never lost control before. He needed to pull free and call a halt to the primitive rush of satisfaction that Lilah had only ever been his.

Lilah moved restlessly beneath him, the subtle shimmy easing the pressure and drawing him deeper. He gritted his teeth. "That's not helping."

Every muscle tensed as Lilah tightened around him, locking him into her body. Incredibly, he felt her climax around him. Burning, irresistible pleasure swamped Zane again. His jaw clenched as his own climax hit him, shoving him over the edge.

Long minutes passed while they lay sprawled together on the couch. Eventually, driven by an electrifying thought, Zane lifted his head.

He could make Lilah pregnant.

Not "could make," he thought grimly. That was something that happened in the future. He was pretty sure they were in the realm of "making pregnant" as in *now*.

Lilah was loathe to move, loathe to separate herself from Zane because she was certain that, as singular and devastatingly pleasurable as the lovemaking had been, despite a little initial discomfort, Zane was less than impressed.

He hadn't liked learning that she was a virgin.

Guilt flooded her when she remembered the shameless way she had clenched around him, holding him in her body.

A reflexive shiver went through her at the memory.

Zane's gaze was oddly flat. "Why didn't you tell me you were a virgin?"

Warm color flooded her cheeks. "There wasn't exactly time for a conversation."

"If I'd known, I would have done things…differently."

"I hadn't exactly planned on this, myself."

He propped himself on his elbows. "Neither had I. Otherwise I would have used a condom. Which is the second issue. How likely are you to get pregnant?"

She felt her flush deepen, although this time the surge of heat wasn't solely because of the very pertinent pregnancy question. "Don't worry, there's no danger of a pregnancy." She tried for a breezy smile, a little difficult when she had just tossed away what her grandmother had always termed her Most Valued Possession. "I take a contraceptive pill."

There was a moment of vibrating silence. Somewhere in the hush of the suite Lilah could hear the ponderous tick of a clock. Outside, somewhere in the distance a siren wailed.

Zane's expression was oddly frozen. "It's a relief someone was in control of the situation. For a minute there I thought we could be parents."

"No chance." She tried not to be riveted by the three very fascinating studs in his lobe. "The one thing I've never planned on being is a single parent."

There was another heavy silence. She got the impression that Zane was not entirely happy with her answer.

"Since you've taken care of the protection so efficiently…" He dipped his head and lightly kissed her then systematically peeled off the chemise. Satisfaction registered in his gaze as he tossed the scrap of silk onto the floor and cupped her breasts, his thumbs sweeping across her nipples.

Lilah's eyes automatically closed as the delicious sensations started all over again.

The rapid shift back into mind-numbing passion set off alarm bells. It occurred to her that now that they had made love, she was in a very precarious position with regard to marriage. Zane was not an option. He had never been an option. His aversion to relationships in general and marriage in particular was well publicized. *She* still wanted marriage, and she couldn't in all good conscience continue with her marriage plans while she had a lover. Regretfully, she did her utmost to dampen down on the desire.

She felt as if she was surfacing from a dream. She had been shameless and had acted with abandon. Her face burned at the memory. She had actively *encouraged* Zane to have unprotected sex with her.

She had clung to him when he had wanted to put a stop to the process and withdraw, then it had been too late and over in seconds.

It was as if, in a weird way, even though she had been sensible enough to guard herself with contraception, a wild, irresponsible part of her had actually courted the very thing she feared most.

Guilt and fatalism churned in her stomach. The sheer weight of her family history and conditioning, the years of guarding against these types of liaisons, should have been enough to stop her.

"We can't do this again." Pressing at Zane's shoulders, she wriggled free, grabbed at her chemise and dragged it on.

Zane's gaze seared over her as she belted the thick robe

around her waist. "All you had to do was say no." The tinge of outrage in his voice stopped her in her tracks.

She flushed guiltily at the truth of that, since she had been the one who hadn't wanted to stop in the first place. She dragged her gaze away from the bronzed, muscular lines of his body as he pulled on dark, fitted trousers. With his strong profile, his black hair tumbling to his broad shoulders, he was beautiful in an untamed, completely masculine way.

Disbelief flooded her that she had actually made love with him. Although the evidence was registering all over her body in tingling aches and the faint stiffening of muscles.

Zane retrieved his shirt. "There's one other thing you don't have to worry about. STD's."

Frowning, Lilah dragged her gaze from the mesmerizing sight of Zane's six-pack.

Zane's gaze snapped to hers. "Sexually transmitted diseases. I don't have any. If tonight was a first for you, it was a first for me. I've never had unprotected sex with a woman before."

Her stomach tightened at the clinical mention of another danger she had failed to consider, and the relegation of their lovemaking to sex. "Um…thanks."

She could feel her face, her whole body, flaming. At twenty-nine, she was probably more naive than the average fifteen-year-old and Zane's reputation with women was legendary. She had been so wrapped up in what she was experiencing she had failed to consider what Zane had to be thinking—that she was hopelessly gauche and naive.

Depression settled around her like a shroud. *Way to go, Lilah Cole. Living up to the family crest. Abandon all thought of responsibility until it's too late.* "If you'll excuse me, I'm going to bed now."

He folded his arms over his chest, his gaze cool. "I'll see you in the morning."

Not if she could help it.

Lilah closed her bedroom door behind her, relieved that

she was finally alone. She checked the bedside clock and an unnerving sense of disorientation set in. It wasn't yet one o'clock. Barely thirty minutes had passed since Zane had walked through the door. Thirty minutes in which her life had drastically altered.

She used her en suite bathroom to freshen up, this time hardly noticing the gorgeous fixtures. Instead of climbing into the elegant four-poster, she changed into jeans, a cotton sweater and sneakers, her fingers fumbling in their haste to get into casual, everyday clothes and restore some semblance of normality.

When she was dressed, she rewound her hair, which had ended up in an untidy mass, into a coil, stabbed pins through to lock the silky strands in place and systematically packed. Twenty minutes after entering her room, she was ready to leave.

Forcing herself to calm down, she sat on the edge of the bed and listened. She had heard Zane's shower earlier, but now the suite was plunged into silence.

Taking a deep breath, she walked to her door and opened it a crack. The sitting room was in darkness. There didn't appear to be any light filtering under the door of Zane's bedroom or flowing out on to the terrace, signaling that he was still awake.

Lifting her bag, she tiptoed to the door and let herself out into the hall. She was almost at the elevator when Spiros loomed out of an alcove and stopped her.

His fractured English almost defeated her. When he picked up his cell and she realized he was going to call Zane, she summoned up a breezy smile, as if the fact that she was sneaking out in the middle of the night was all part of the plan. "Nessuno." She jabbed at the call button and carefully enunciated each word as she spoke. "No need to call Zane, he's sleeping."

He frowned then nodded, clearly not happy.

Forty minutes later, Lilah paid off the taxi that had delivered her back to her apartment and walked inside.

She checked the messages on her phone. They were all

from tabloids and women's magazines wanting interviews. She had expected that Spiros, who had been uneasy about the fact that she had left at such an odd hour, would have caved and woken Zane up. Clearly, that hadn't happened, because there was no message from Zane.

Feeling oddly let down that she hadn't heard from Zane, she deleted them all.

Pulling the drapes tight, just in case someone was lurking outside with a camera, she changed into a spare chemise in pitch darkness and fell into bed.

She slept fitfully, waking at dawn, half expecting the phone to ring, or for Zane to be thumping on her door.

She got up and made a cup of tea, collapsed on the couch and watched movies. By ten o'clock, when Zane hadn't either called or come by, exhausted from waiting, she dropped back into bed and slept until two in the afternoon.

When she got up, her stomach growling with hunger, she checked her phone. There were a string of new messages but, again, they were all from reporters.

Stabbing the delete button, she erased them all and finally decided to put herself out of her misery by taking the phone off the hook. On impulse, she checked her cell phone, but it wasn't in her bag. She must have left it in Zane's suite.

To keep the cold misery at bay that Zane didn't appear to have any interest in contacting her, she opened a can of soup and made toast. Evan knocked on her door, wanting to return her spare key and check that she was okay. At four o'clock a second visitor knocked.

A courier. He handed her a package and requested she sign for it.

She scribbled her name, closed the door then ripped the package open. Her stomach dropped like a stone as her fingers closed around her cell phone.

From the second she had left Zane's suite, she realized, she had been waiting for him to come after her, to insist that he wanted her back. That what they had shared had been as special for him as it had been for her.

That clearly wasn't the case.

Zane hadn't even bothered to include a note with the phone. All he had done was return her property in such a way that made it clear he no longer wanted contact.

Feeling numb, she put the phone on charge. Almost immediately, it beeped. Crazy hope gripped her as she opened the message.

It was Lucas, not Zane. He wanted her to call him.

Using the cell, she put the call through. Lucas picked up immediately. The conversation was brief. Thanks to her boosted media profile, she had just won a prestigious design award in Milan, which would give Ambrosi an edge in the market. A week ago, she had applied for the job of managing the new Ambrosi Pearl facility, which was to be constructed on the island of Ambrus, one of the smaller islands in the Medinian group. If she wanted the job, it was hers.

The job was a promotion with a substantial raise in her salary plus a generous living allowance. If she took it, paying her mother's mortgage would no longer be a problem. She would even be able to save.

The only problem was, Zane lived on Medinos. Although, with the amount of travel he did, most of it to the States, she doubted their paths would often cross.

A bonus would be that she could leave Sydney and all of the media hype behind. She would have a fresh start.

Away from her latest sex scandal.

Taking a deep breath, she took the plunge and affirmed that she would take the job.

Lucas rang back a few minutes later. He had booked a flight, leaving in two days. Her accommodation, until a house could be arranged, was the Atraeus Resort on Medinos.

Reeling from the sudden change of direction her life had taken, Lilah rang her mother and told her the good news, carefully glossing over the bad parts.

After she had hung up, she cleared her answering machine and disconnected the phone. She also turned her cell phone off. She didn't know how long it would take the media to discover that Lucas had offered her a job on Medinos, but given the added hype behind the Milan award, she didn't think it would take long.

Too wound up to try and relax again, she decided to take one of her finished paintings to the gallery that handled her work.

When she walked into the trendy premises, the proprietor, Quincy Travers, a plump, balding man with a shrewd glint in his eyes, greeted her with open arms.

With glee he took the abstract she'd painted and handed her a check for an astounding amount. "As soon as I saw the story in the paper I contacted some collectors I know and put an extra couple of zeroes on the price of the paintings. I sold out within thirty minutes."

"Great." Lilah's delight at the check, which was enough to pay off her mother's mortgage and still leave change, went into the same deep, dark hole that had snuffed out her delight at the Milan award and her promotion.

She shoved the check in her purse. Just what she needed to brighten her day. Like her jewelry design, any value her art now had was tied to her notoriety.

Quincy propped the painting on an empty display easel and rubbed his hands together. "No need to put a price on this. I've got buyers waiting. Sex sells. What else have you got, love? You could scribble with crayons and we'd still make a fortune."

"Actually, I'm leaving town for a while, so that will be the last one for the foreseeable future."

Quincy looked crestfallen. "If I'd known that, I would have asked more for the other paintings." He rummaged beneath his counter and came up with a battered address book. "But all is not lost. If the buyers know this is the last one, they'll pay." He flipped it open and reached for his phone. "By the way, did you really, er, *date* both brothers at the same time?"

Lilah could feel herself turning pink. She was suddenly fiercely glad she was leaving town in two days. "No." Ducking her head, she walked quickly out of the gallery.

She had just slept with the one.

Nine

Two days later, fresh off a flight from Broome in Western Australia and frustrated that he had not been able to get any reply from either Lilah's work or home phone, or cell, Zane swung the Corvette into the parking space outside her building.

He buzzed the apartment. While he waited for a response, the electrifying moments on the couch replayed in his mind. The enthusiastic way Lilah had clung to him, the explosive moment when he had known for sure that she had never made love with Lucas, Peters or any other man. The fierce way she had locked him into her body when he had attempted to withdraw, as if she hadn't wanted to let him go.

The brain freeze that had hit him, because he hadn't wanted to stop, either.

When he'd discovered that Lilah had sneaked out on him during the night, he had been both furious and relieved.

The fact that he had made the monumental mistake of making love to her without protection, that he could have made her pregnant, still stunned him.

It had been right up there with finding out that she had been a virgin.

A day spent kicking his heels, trying to decide if those out-of-control moments had been unscripted and spontaneous or if he had been neatly manipulated by a consummate operator had been enough.

Every time he had examined what had happened, he had come to the same inescapable conclusion. Whatever Lilah's motives had been in surrendering her virginity to him, she had taken care of the contraception, which argued her innocence.

He had done a background check on Lilah, even going so far as to fly to her hometown, Broome. When he'd found out that, like him, she was illegitimate, several pieces of the puzzle that was Lilah Cole had fallen into place.

He knew how a dysfunctional upbringing could influence decisions. Lilah had been brought up by her single mother, whose health was poor. Consequently, the financial burden had now fallen on her. She not only paid her own costs in Sydney, she paid her mother's mortgage and medical bills.

The knowledge put Lilah's search for a well-heeled husband into an irritatingly practical light. It had also exposed how potentially vulnerable Lilah could be to an "arrangement" should some man try to step into her life.

He leaned on the buzzer again. Since Lilah wasn't answering any calls, he had reasoned that she had most probably taken some time off work and was inside, hiding out from the press.

His frustration level increasing when there was still no response, he cut through the adjacent property, another shabby warehouse, and pushed through the broken fence into Lilah's backyard.

He examined the bifold doors and windows, which were locked and blanked out by thick drapes. He rapped on the door and tried calling. When there was no answer he walked back around to the front door and pressed buzzers until he got an answer from one of the other apartments.

A voice like a rusty nail being slowly extracted from a sheet of iron informed him that Lilah had left the country. Her apartment was now empty, if he wanted to rent it.

Zane terminated the conversation and strode back to the Corvette. A quick call to Lucas answered the question that was threatening to aggravate his newly discovered anger problem.

"Lilah has flown to Medinos. She's agreed to head up the new Ambrosi Pearls facility."

Zane's fingers tightened on his cell. "Who made the arrangement?"

"I did. I'll be flying out to Medinos in the next few days to check that she's settling in."

A snapping sound informed Zane that he had just broken one of the hinges that attached the LCD screen to the body of his phone. "Carla won't be happy."

That was an understatement. Carla Ambrosi was known for her passionate outbursts. But whatever Carla might feel about Lucas's continuing involvement with Lilah didn't come close to Zane's level of unhappiness.

"After the crazy stuff the tabloids have been printing," Lucas said grimly, "the less Carla knows about Lilah the better. I'm organizing for her to spend some time with her mother here when I fly out to Medinos."

Zane's stomach tightened. Which meant Carla would be conveniently out of the way for Lucas's meeting with Lilah. "When did Lilah leave?"

"Today."

Zane terminated the conversation and placed a call to Elena. Within seconds she had located the information he wanted. The only flight out of Sydney to Medinos that day had already departed.

Tossing the phone on the passenger seat, Zane slid behind the wheel and accelerated away from the curb. Lilah had left that morning, but her flight was long, with a three-hour stopover in Singapore and another shorter stop in Dubai. Using the Atraeus private jet, he would easily reach Medinos before her.

Whatever ideas his brother might have of conducting a clandestine affair with Lilah, Zane was certain of one fact. Lilah hadn't chosen to give herself to Lucas; she had given herself to him.

He, also, had made a choice when he had made love with Lilah. He wanted her, and after two years, one night had not been enough. One thing was certain: he was not about to let Lucas entice Lilah away.

Satisfaction curled in his stomach as the decision settled in. If he'd had any reservations, in that moment they were gone.

The complication of Lilah's virginity and marriage plan aside, he was finally going to live up to the reputation of his marauding ancestor.

Lilah was his, and he was taking her.

Lilah stepped into the air-conditioned terminal on Medinos.

Almost immediately she was accosted by a uniformed security guard, a holstered gun on one thigh.

Exhausted from the long nerve-racking flight, during which she had only been able to sleep in snatches, she accompanied the officer to a small, sterile interview room. Several fruitless questions later, because the guard's English was limited and her Medinian was close to nonexistent, she resigned herself to wait. The one piece of information she had gleaned was that, apparently, they were waiting for a member of the Atraeus family.

Minutes later, her frustration levels rising, her luggage, along with a foam cup of coffee, was delivered to the interview room and an airport official showed up to personally process her arrival papers. As the official handed her stamped passport back, the door opened. Zane, dressed in dark jeans and a loose white shirt, his hair ruffled as if he'd dragged his fingers through it repeatedly, strolled into the room.

For a confused moment Lilah had difficulty grasping that

Zane was actually here, then the meaning of his presence sank in. "You're the Atraeus who had me detained."

The official left, the door closing quietly behind him.

Zane frowned. "Who were you expecting? Lucas?"

The flatness of Zane's voice was faintly shocking. Lilah couldn't help thinking it was a long way from the teasing grin and the seductive huskiness of Saturday night. "As far as I know, Lucas is still in Sydney."

Zane placed a newspaper, which had been tucked under one arm, down on the desktop.

The glaring headline, *Lucas Atraeus Installs Mistress on Isle of Medinos,* made her bristle. When she had flown out of Sydney, she had hoped she was leaving all of that behind.

Folding the paper over, she threw it in the trashcan beside the desk. "I haven't seen that one. They don't hand out Sydney gossip sheets as part of the in-flight entertainment."

Zane perched on the edge of the desk, arms folded across his chest. "Who knew that you were flying out to Medinos?"

Lilah located her handbag and stored her passport in a secure pocket. Making a quick exit lugging a large suitcase, a carry-on bag, her laptop and her handbag would be difficult, but she was ready to give it a go. "Quite a lot of people. It wasn't a secret."

Zane looked briefly irritated as she tried to harness her laptop to the suitcase using a set of buckles that was clearly inadequate for the job. "That's not helpful."

"It wasn't meant to be." She hauled on a dainty strap and finally had the laptop secure.

"So who do you think could have leaked the information that you were moving to Medinos to the press?"

She moved on to the carry-on case, which posed a problem. She was going to need a trolley after all.

"You don't have to worry about the luggage. I'll carry it for you."

Anger flowed through her at the implication that *she* could have sold the story. "I prefer to manage on my own."

"You don't have to, since I'm here to pick you up." With efficient movements, Zane unhooked the laptop and used the straps to neatly attach the carry-on case to the large suitcase.

Lilah reclaimed her laptop. "I don't get it. You didn't come around or call, and now—"

"I called. Your phone didn't seem to be working."

She tried to get her tired brain around the astounding fact that Zane hadn't abandoned her, entirely. Although, there was nothing loverlike about his demeanor now. A lightbulb went on in her head. "Don't tell me you thought I could have leaked the story because I'm angling to be Lucas's mistress?"

"Or to break Lucas and Carla up."

For a vibrating moment she struggled against the desire to empty what was left of her coffee down his front. Instead, she set her laptop down and, stepping close, ran her finger down Zane's chest, pausing over the steady thud of his heart. "Why would I, when as you so eloquently put it, I've already got the real thing?"

Heat flared in his gaze. His fingers closed around her wrist, trapping her palm against the wall of his chest. "Past tense, Lilah. You were the one who walked out."

Shock reverberated through her that he could possibly have wanted her to stay. "I didn't think you were…serious."

His gaze was unnervingly steady. "One-night stands are not exactly my thing."

The heat from his chest burned into her palm. "So all those stories in the press about you and who knows how many gorgeous women are untrue?"

His free hand curled around her nape. He reeled her in a little closer. "Mostly."

Honest, but still dangerous. Distantly, she registered that this was what she had so badly wanted from Zane two days ago. He had finally come after her and in true pirate fashion was seemingly intent on dragging her back to bed. "So, in theory then, the press could have lied about me."

He leaned forward; his lips feathered her jaw sending a hot tingle of sensation through her. "It's possible."

"I'm not interested in breaking Lucas and Carla up."

"Good, because I have a proposition for you." He bit down gently on her lobe. "Two days on an island paradise. You and me."

Sensation shimmered through her, briefly blanking her mind. So that was what it was like, she thought a little breathlessly. She had read that the earlobe was an erogenous zone. Now, finally, she could attest to that fact.

She took a deep breath and let it out slowly. The idea of an exciting interlude with Zane before she started work and became once more embroiled in her search for a stable, trustworthy husband, was unbearably seductive. There were no good reasons to go, only bad ones. "Yes."

She caught the quick flash of his grin before his mouth closed on hers, and for long seconds she forgot to breathe.

Ten minutes later, Lilah found herself installed in the rear seat of a limousine, Zane beside her and the familiar figure of Spiros behind the wheel. A short drive later and they pulled into a picturesque marina.

She examined the ranks of gleaming superyachts, launches and sailboats tied up to a neat series of jetties. "This doesn't look like the Atraeus Resort."

"It's a nice day. I thought you might enjoy the boat ride."

Spiros opened her door, distracting her. When she turned back to Zane, the seat next to her was empty. Zane was already out of the limousine, his jacket off and draped over one shoulder. Following suit, she climbed out, wincing at the dazzling brightness of sunlight reflecting off white boats. Finding her sunglasses, she slid them onto the bridge of her nose.

By that time, Spiros, who she had noticed had not met her gaze once during the last few minutes, had her cases out of the trunk. Zane was already halfway down the jetty and untying ropes. The boat trip to the resort seemed to be a fait accompli, so Lilah followed in Spiros's wake, determined to enjoy the sunny day and the spectacular sea views.

By the time she reached the sleek white yacht, her cases were already stowed. Zane extended his hand and helped her climb aboard.

Almost instantly the engine hummed to life. Spiros walked along the jetty, released the last rope and tossed it over the stern. Lilah couldn't help noticing that he seemed to be in a hurry. When he didn't climb aboard she frowned. "Isn't Spiros coming?"

"Not on this trip." With deft skill, Zane maneuvered the yacht out of its berth.

Minutes later, they cleared the marina and the boat picked up speed, wallowing slightly in the chop. Feeling faintly queasy with the motion, Lilah sat down and tried to enjoy the scenery.

Twenty minutes later, her unease turned to suspicion. Instead of hugging the coastline they seemed to be heading for open sea. The coastline of Medinos had receded, and the island of Ambrus loomed ahead.

Dragging strands of hair out of her eyes, she pushed to her feet, gripping the back of her seat to stay upright. "This is not the way to the resort."

"I'm taking you to Ambrus."

"There's nothing *on* Ambrus."

His gaze rested briefly on hers. "That's not strictly true. There's an unfinished resort on the northern headland."

The yacht rounded a point and sailed into calmer water. Lilah stared at the curve of the beach ahead and the tumbled wreckage of the old pearl facility, which had been destroyed in the Second World War. It was, literally, a bombsite. In a flash, Spiros's odd behavior and his hurried exit made sense. Zane had planned this. She gestured at the looming beach. "I didn't agree to that. You said two days. Paradise."

Zane throttled back on the engine. "Maybe I wasn't talking about the scenery."

An instant flashback to the heated few minutes on Zane's couch made her blush. "I didn't exactly find paradise in your hotel room."

"There wasn't time. If you'll recall, you ran out on me."

Her jaw firmed. When she had landed on Medinos her life had been firmly under control. Somehow in the space of an hour everything had gone to hell in a handbasket again. "I'm booked in at the Atraeus Resort. That's where I'm staying for the next few weeks."

"You agreed. Two days." His jaw tightened. "Or did you want another media furor when Lucas arrives tomorrow?"

She stared at the tough line of his jaw. The dazzling few moments in the customs interview room when she'd been weak enough to allow him to kiss her replayed in her mind. That had been her first mistake. "I assumed you were taking me to my suite at the Atraeus Resort."

"I apologize for the deception," he said bluntly, although there was no hint of apology in his gaze. "I'll take you to Medinos in two days' time. Once Lucas leaves."

She stared at the deserted stretch of coastline then back at the distant view of Medinos. She had wanted out of the media circus and she had wanted peace and quiet. It looked like now she was getting both, with a vengeance. "Is there power, an internet connection?"

"There's a generator. No internet."

"Then we need to go back to Medinos. I'll be missed. People will be concerned. Questions will be asked."

Zane frowned. "Who, exactly, is going to ask these questions?"

Lilah stared fixedly at the horizon, aware that the conversation had drifted into dangerous waters. "I have…friends."

"It's only two days."

A little desperate now, Lilah tried for a vague look. "Online friends. I need to keep in touch."

Zane's gaze was unnervingly piercing. "And being away from an internet connection for two days is an issue?"

She crossed her arms over her chest, refusing to be drawn. "It could be."

After the disappointment with Lucas she had felt an urgency to move along with her marriage project and had committed to a series of dates with her list of potentially perfect husbands. Howard had only been the first. Up until that moment she had been too busy with making arrangements to leave Sydney, and preparing herself for a new life and a new job, to stop and think about the upcoming series of dates she had arranged for a scheduled holiday back home in two weeks' time.

The sound of the engine changed as they neared shore. The reality of what was happening sank in as the huge, deserted sweep of the crescent bay underlined their complete isolation. "You're kidnapping me."

Zane's brows jerked together. "That's a little dramatic. We're staying at a beach house where we can spend some time together, uninterrupted."

Against all the odds her heart thumped wildly at his bad-tempered, rather blunt statement, which definitely indicated a desire to keep her to himself. She guessed she could excuse him, although not right away.

He had *kidnapped* her.

She clamped down on the dizzying delight that he wanted her enough to actually commit a crime. After Zane's behavior in Sydney and her misery when he had failed to come after her, it was a scenario she hadn't dared consider.

The engine dropped to a low hum. Zane stabbed at a button. The rattle of a chain cut through the charged silence as he dropped anchor.

Lilah watched the grim set of Zane's shoulders as he studied the chain for a few seconds to make sure the anchor had taken hold. "I suppose on Medinos, trying to get a conviction against an Atraeus is impossible."

Zane went very still. When he straightened, she realized

the faint shaking of his shoulders was laughter. He grinned, suddenly looking rakish. "Not impossible, just highly improbable."

Ten

The inflatable boat scraped ashore on the pristine white-sand beach. With a fluid movement, Zane climbed out and held it steady against the wash of waves. Ignoring the hand he offered her, Lilah clambered over the side, shoes in one hand, handbag gripped in the other.

Ankle-deep water splashed her calves, surprisingly cold as she stepped onto the firmly packed sand at the shoreline. With muscular ease, Zane pulled the inflatable higher on the beach, unwound rope and tied it to an iron ring attached to a weathered post.

Shielding her eyes from the sun, which was almost directly overhead, Lilah examined the bay. Beyond the post was an expanse of tussock grass interspersed with darker patches of wild thyme and rosemary. Farther back, and to the right, she could see, following the broad curve of an estuary, the remains of sheds. To the right, flanked by a grove of gnarled olive trees, was the ivy-encrusted remnant of what must have once been a grand villa. She instantly knew that this had to be

Sebastien Ambrosi's villa. Sienna and Carla Ambrosi's grand-father had left Medinos in the 1940s and settled in Broome, Australia, where he had reestablished the Ambrosi Pearls business. "The house looks smaller than I imagined."

"You knew Sebastien Ambrosi?"

"My mother used to work for him in Broome, seeding and grading pearls. He was very kind to us." She lifted her shoulders. "I've always been fascinated by Ambrosi Pearls, and I've always longed to see Ambrus."

While Zane unloaded their cases, she walked along the beach. From here nothing was visible except the misty line where sea met sky, no land, no Medinos or any other island, just water and isolation.

She studied the Atraeus beach house, which was set back into a curve in the jagged cliffs. Built on three levels, it wasn't, by any stretch of the imagination, a cottage. Planes of glass glinted in the sun. The teaklike wood and the jutting curves and angles gave it the appearance of a gigantic ship flowing out of the rock. Sited higher than the beach, it no doubt commanded a magnificent view.

"Are you all right?"

She whirled. "You're holding me prisoner. Other than that, I guess everything is just fine."

Any hint of amusement winked out of his gaze. "You are not a 'prisoner.' I've asked a Medinian couple, Jorge and Marta, to stay over for a couple of days. Jorge is a trained butler, and Marta is a chef. I'm trying to keep this as PC as I can."

"A PC kidnapping."

His jaw set in an obdurate line. "If you're hungry, Marta will have lunch ready up at the house."

Zane breathed a sigh of relief when Lilah appeared, fresh and cool after showering and changing into a white shift, to join him on one of the enormous decks for lunch.

Marta had set out a tempting array of salads and meats. As Zane watched Lilah eat, curiously at home in the wild setting, a sense of possessiveness filled him.

The house on Ambrus was a luxury retreat. He could have brought any number of women he had known here, but he had never been even remotely tempted. Lilah was his first guest. Not that she had seen it that way.

He realized he wasn't just attracted to Lilah; he liked her, even down to the way she pushed his buttons. She had given him a hard time from the minute he had caught up with her in the airport.

His decision to do whatever it took to keep her with him settled in. She wasn't ready to admit it yet, or surrender to him, but he was confident he could change that. Deny it as she might, she couldn't hide the fact that she wanted him.

Until that moment, he hadn't known how this would work, but now the equation was simple. Lucas had had his chance, and made his choice. He was no longer prepared to allow his brother, or any other man, near her.

Emotion expanded in his chest. After living an admittedly wild, single life, it was something of a U-turn. Until that moment he hadn't known how much he wanted to make it. He still didn't know how exactly they would work out a relationship, how long it would last—or if Lilah was even prepared to try, given her agenda—but he was finally prepared to try.

Lilah placed her fork down and smothered a yawn. "I think I'll go take a nap."

Zane watched her walk back into the house and determinedly squashed the desire to go after her.

After detaining her at the airport then kidnapping her, carrying her to bed would not improve on the impression he had made. Given that he wanted more than a short-lived liaison, he needed to take a different, more mature, approach.

As much as he wanted to follow up on the promise of those rushed few moments on the couch, he would have to wait.

She didn't trust him yet. At this point trust was a commodity neither of them possessed.

When Lilah woke, the sun had gone down and she could smell something savory cooking. Pushing back the sheet, which was the only covering she had needed in the balmy heat, she walked through to the lavish marble en suite bathroom to freshen up.

It seemed that even when the Atraeus family holidayed at the beach, it was done with style. After washing her face, she ran a comb through her hair and coiled it into a loose knot on top of her head. Eyes narrowed, she surveyed her crumpled wardrobe. If she was launching herself into a two-day venture of passion, she needed to dress the part.

In the end she changed into a simple but elegant ivory cotton dress with an intriguingly low cut neckline that she usually teamed with a thin silk camisole.

She inserted pearl studs in her ears and spent a good ten minutes on her makeup. The results weren't exactly spectacular, but Zane hadn't given her much notice. Feeling buoyed up but more than a little on edge, she strolled out to the main sitting room.

For the next two days she had a guilty kind of permission to put her marriage plans to one side and immerse herself in a passionate experience. Unfortunately, she was going to have to play it by ear. Nothing in her extensive research on dating with a view to marriage had prepared her to cope with a rampant love affair with a totally unsuitable man.

Zane was already on the deck dressed in fitted dark pants that outlined the muscular length of his legs and a loose, gauzy white shirt. On another man the semitransparent shirt might have looked soft and effeminate, but on Zane the effect of muslin clinging to broad shoulders was powerful and utterly masculine. With his hair sleeked back in a ponytail, the studs in his ear were clearly visible, making him look even more like his piratical ancestor.

Somewhere classical music played softly. Marta had set the table, but this time it was glamorously romantic with white damask, gleaming gold cutlery and ornate gold candlesticks. Lit candles provided a soft, flickering glow, highlighting the Lalique glassware. With the deck floating in darkness above the rocks and the sea luminous and gleaming below, it was easy to fantasize that she was standing in the prow of a ship.

Dinner was a gazpacho-style soup with fresh, warm rolls, followed by a rich chicken casserole with pasta. Desert was a platter of honeyed pastries, fresh figs and soft white cheese.

Marta and Jorge cleared away. When Zane indicated they should go inside, she preceded him gladly, grateful for the distraction from the growing awareness that they were finally alone.

Feeling even more nervous now, Lilah walked around the huge sitting room, studying the artwork on the walls. She stopped at a beautifully executed watercolor of a rocky track, which culminated in a cave.

Zane's deep, cool voice close to her ear sent a tingling jolt of awareness through her. "That came from the old villa. One of the few possessions that survived the World War Two bombing."

She forced herself to study the familiar signature at the bottom right-hand corner of the painting, although with Zane behind her she was now utterly distracted. "Of course, one of Sebastien's."

"You might recognize a couple of landmarks." He reached past her to indicate a familiar headland, then farther in the background, a high peak. "It's a painting of an area behind the old villa."

She tensed at Zane's proximity. It was ridiculous to be so on edge. It wasn't as if they hadn't kissed a number of times, made love.

The warmth of his breath on her nape sent a shivery frisson down her spine. "Would you like a drink?"

When she turned, he had already moved away and was at the drinks cabinet, a decanter of brandy in one hand, a balloon glass in the other. "No. Thanks."

He splashed brandy in the glass and gestured at the comfortable leather couches. "Have a seat.

Lilah chose an armchair close to the fire, sank into the

cloud of leather and tried to relax. She blushed when she registered Zane's gaze lingering in the area of her neckline, and tried to brazen out the moment.

"Why didn't you tell me that Peters was gay?"

She stiffened at the question. "And how would you know that?"

"I was interested. I made a few inquiries."

Outrage stiffened her spine. She knew what Zane did for a living. He was The Atraeus Group's fixer. If there was a difficult situation or a problem with personnel, Zane took care of it along with a sinister clutch of characters, one of whom happened to be Spiros. "You mean you had me, and Evan, investigated."

Irritation gleamed in his dark eyes. "I asked a few questions in the Ambrosi office. That girl who works in PR? What's her name?"

"Lisa."

"That's it. She told me."

Lilah let out a breath. She should have guessed. Lisa, who was a romantic at heart, would have been dazzled by Zane. She would have hemorrhaged information in the belief that Zane was truly interested in Lilah. "I agreed to be Evan's date on a few occasions to help him keep up the charade that he was straight for his accounting firm, that's all."

Zane positioned himself to one side of the fireplace, the brandy balloon cradled in one hand. "And what about Evan's boss?"

Her mind flashed back to a moment at the charity's annual art auction two years ago when Zane had found her fending off Britten after she had asked him a few leading questions on the subject of marriage and he had gotten the wrong idea.

"I thought you were involved with both Peters and Britten."

"Climbing the corporate ladder?" Which explained why he had practically ignored her for two years.

"Something like that." He finished his brandy and set the glass down on the mantel.

Lilah kept her gaze glued on the flames. "And after we made love, when you knew I hadn't slept with Evan or Britten, or Lucas, why didn't you bother to contact me?"

"I figured we both needed some time. Besides, I needed to go out of town. Broome, to be exact."

Lilah's head came up at the mention of her hometown. "To check out the pearl farms?"

"I wasn't interested in the pearls on that trip. I went to see your mother. I needed her permission."

For a moment she actually considered that Zane had done something crazily old-fashioned and had declared his intention to ask for her hand. Almost instantly she squashed that idea. Firstly, he hadn't asked her anything remotely like that, and since he'd walked into the interview room at the airport there had been plenty of time. Secondly, he would have to both want her *and* love her to propose marriage. "Permission to do what?"

"To pay off your mother's mortgage and outstanding loans."

She shot to her feet, any idea of a romantic idyll gone. "You've got no right to meddle in my family affairs, or offer my mother money."

"The agreement has nothing to do with you and me. Or our relationship."

"We don't *have* a relationship, and my mother is in no position to repay you."

"I don't want the money back."

She went still inside. "What do you want, then?"

"I already have it. Peace of mind."

She frowned. "How can paying off my mother's house give you peace of mind?"

"Because it takes financial pressure off you. Your mother was worried about you." Reaching into his pocket, he produced a slip of paper.

Lilah recognized the check she had written out and expressed to her mother so she could make arrangements with her bank to pay off her mortgage. Clearly, the check had never been cashed.

He dropped the check on the coffee table. "You can give that back to Lucas."

The coolness of his voice jerked her chin up. "It isn't Lucas's money. Although indirectly he, and you, did help me earn it."

Zane's brows jerked together. "The money didn't come from Ambrosi, I made sure of that."

"No. Some of my paintings sold. With the notoriety of my being involved with Lucas, then you, the gallery owner put huge prices on the works and sold out in one day." She picked up the check. "This was the result."

He took it from her fingers, crumpled it in his fist and tossed it into the fire. "Do you know what it did to me to see that check? I thought Lucas was helping you out financially."

Lilah was on her feet now. "And that it was…what? Some kind of down payment on my becoming his mistress?"

"Maybe not right now, but it could have been, eventually."

She let out a breath and tried to calm down. So…okay. She could understand his thinking, because she knew something of his background. She knew his mother had fallen from the glamorous life of an A-list party girl into drug addiction and had depended on a string of less than A-list men to support her and her son. It had been a precarious existence, and Zane had been forced to live it until he was fourteen. "What I don't get is, why you could think that?"

He stepped close and threaded his fingers through her hair. She felt the pins give, moments later her hair slipped down around her shoulders. "You traveled to Medinos for a first date with Lucas. Now you're here, a resident, and Lucas is planning on having a couple of days on Medinos…without his bride-to-be."

She frowned. "Lucas is my boss, that's all. The only thing I really liked about him was that he looks like you."

The bald statement hung in the air, surprising her almost as much as it surprised Zane.

"You hardly knew me."

She gripped the lapels of his shirt and absently worked a button loose. "But then that's how it works."

Zane tilted her face so she was looking directly at him. "You're losing me."

"Fatal attraction. The *coup de foudre,* the clap of thunder."

"Still lost."

"Sex," she muttered baldly. "As in…an affair."

His expression turned grim. He released his grip on her. "A dangerously unstable affair. With a younger man."

She blinked at the grim note in his voice. "Uh—more or less."

A split second later she was free altogether and Zane was several feet away, gripping the back of a leather chair. "Before we go any further let's get one thing clear. I didn't bring you here for a quick, meaningless thrill. If you want me to make love to you, we're going to go about it in a normal, rational, *adult* way."

Instead of throwing herself at him like some desperate, love-starved teenager. The way she had the last time.

The way she had been about to do about thirty seconds ago.

Lilah's cheeks burned. Zane was still gripping the back of the chair. As if *he* needed the protection.

She had known this was going to be a sticky area, and she had messed up, again. She was beginning to understand what had gone so disastrously wrong for Cole women over the years. With their naturally passionate natures they tried too hard to be "good" then got caught in an uncontrollable whiplash of desire. "Now that you mention it, I don't think this is the greatest time to make love."

His gaze was as cool and steady as if those heated moments had never happened. "Then, good night. If you need anything, I'm just down the hall. Or, if you prefer, you can call on Jorge and Marta who are sleeping in the downstairs apartment, although they don't speak any English."

The words *But what if I change my mind?* balanced on the tip of her tongue. She hastily withdrew them as he padded across to the ornate liquor cabinet and splashed more brandy into a clean glass.

She had already made a string of rash decisions with regard to Zane. Before she made even more of a fool of herself, she needed to think things through.

Although the fact that she *was* going to make a fool of herself again was suddenly, glaringly, obvious.

Eleven

The following morning, Lilah woke, exhausted and heavy-eyed after a night spent tossing and turning.

She had lain awake for hours, listening to the sounds of the sea and Zane's footsteps when he had finally gone to bed in the small hours. Aware of Zane, a short distance away in the next bedroom, she had eventually dropped off, only to wake periodically, thump her pillow into shape and try to sleep again.

Kicking the sheet aside, she padded to her bathroom and stared at her pale face and tangled hair in the mirror.

Zane's withdrawal had created an odd reversal in her mind. Sexually, the ball was in her court. If she wanted him, it was clear she would have to make the first move. No more excuses or deception about who was driving what.

His demand had succeeded in focusing her mind. Now, instead of trying to talk herself out of a wild fling with Zane, she was consumed with how, exactly, one went about asking a man for sex.

Lilah showered and dressed in a white camisole and a pair of board shorts, a bikini beneath, in case she felt like a swim.

After applying sunscreen, she walked out to the kitchen, only to discover that the nervous tension that had dogged her all morning had been unnecessary. Zane had left the house early. According to Marta's gestures and the few words Lilah could recognize, he had gone sailing.

Feeling relieved and deflated at the same time, she walked out on the deck where the table was set for breakfast. One glance at the empty sweep of the bay confirmed that the yacht was gone.

After breakfast she walked down to the beach and went for a swim. After sunbathing until she was dry, she walked back to the house, showered off the salt and changed back into the camisole and boardies.

To fill in time, she strolled through the house, examining the art on the walls, pausing at the watercolor that had been done by Sebastien Ambrosi.

Zane had said the painting was an actual place on the island, behind the villa. From the distant peaks included in the landscape, the cave was set on high ground. On impulse, she decided to see if she could find the cave and, at the same time, see if her cell phone would work.

Pulling on a pair of trainers, she slipped her cell in a pocket and indicated to Marta that she was going to walk to the place in the painting.

A few minutes exploring around the old villa site and she found the entrance to a narrow track that ran up through the steep hills behind the villa.

Twenty minutes of intermittent walking and climbing and she topped a rise. The view was magnificent. In the distance she could even make out hazy peaks that formed part of the mountainous inland region of Medinos. She hadn't seen any evidence of the cave.

Sitting down on a rocky outcropping, she tried the phone, but the screen continued to glow with a "No Service" message.

Instead of feeling trapped and frustrated, she felt oddly

relieved. She had done her duty, attempted to make contact with the outside world, and had failed.

She was clambering down a steep, rocky slope when she saw Zane's yacht dropping anchor in the bay. Her heart skipped a beat as she watched Zane toss the inflatable over the side. In the same instant her foot slipped. A sharp pain shot up her ankle. She tried to correct her footing and ended up sliding the rest of the way down the bank.

Sucking in a breath, she tested her ankle, the same one she'd turned in Sydney. Annoyed with the injury, which, while minor, would make the trip down slow, she began to hobble in an effort to walk off the injury.

It started to rain. She was congratulating herself on traversing the narrowest, most precipitous part of the track with steep slopes on both sides, when she glimpsed Zane walking toward her and slipped again, this time landing flat on her back. She lay on the wet ground, eyes closed against the pelting rain, and counted to ten. When her lids flipped open, Zane was staring down at her, water dripping from his chin, wet T-shirt plastered to his torso faithfully outlining every ridge and muscle. "Two days. Paradise, you said."

"It would have been if we'd spent the time in bed."

"Huh." She pushed into a sitting position and checked her ankle and in the process realized that the white camisole she was wearing was now practically invisible.

Zane crouched down beside her. Lean brown fingers closed around her ankle.

"Ouch. Don't touch it." Despite the slight tenderness, a jolt of purely sensual awareness shot through her.

His expression was irritatingly calm. "It's not swollen, so it can't be too sore. How did you do it?"

"I saw you and slipped. Twice."

The accusation bounced off him. "Can you walk?"

"Yes."

"Too bad." He pulled her up until she was balanced on one foot then swung her into his arms.

The rain began to pelt down. She clutched at his shoulders. "I'm heavy."

He glanced pointedly at her chest. "There are compensations."

He continued on down the hill but instead of taking a broad track to the beach, he veered left heading for a dark tumble of rocks. They rounded a corner and a low opening became visible. "Sebastien's cave."

"I thought it might be near."

The mouth to the cave was broad, allowing light to flow into the cavern. Ducking to avoid the rock overhang, Zane set Lilah down on one of the boulders that littered the opening. He shrugged out of the rucksack he had strapped to his back, unfastened the waterproof flap and extracted a flashlight. The bright beam cut through the gloom, revealing a dusty brass lantern balanced on a natural rock shelf and an equally dusty brass lighter lying beside it.

He crouched down and examined her ankle again. "A bandage would help."

She retracted her ankle from his tingling grip. "I can wait for a bandage. Really, it isn't that bad."

"Bad enough that it's starting to swell." He peeled out of his T-shirt.

Murky light gleamed on ridged abs and muscled pecs, the darker striations of the two thin scars that crisscrossed his abdomen. One was shorter and lighter, as if it hadn't been so serious, the other more defined and longer, curling just above one hip.

She dragged her gaze from the mesmerizing expanse of bronzed, sculpted muscle, abruptly aware that he knew exactly the effect he was having on her and that he was enjoying it. "Don't you need to wear that?"

"It's either my T-shirt or your top. You choose."

She concentrated on keeping her gaze rigidly on the wadded T-shirt. "Yours."

"Thought you'd say that."

Using his teeth, he ripped a small hole near the hem of the shirt then tore a broad strip, working the tear until he ended up with a continuous run of bandage. Clasping her calf, he began to firmly wind the bandage around her ankle.

"Don't tell me, you were a Boy Scout."

"Sea Scout." He ripped the trailing end of the bandage into two strips and tied it off.

"*Ouch*. Figures."

He wound a finger in a damp strand of her hair and tugged. "Goes with the pirate image?"

She reclaimed her hair and tried to repress the brazen impulse to wallow in the jolt of killer charm and flirt back. "Yes."

Rising to his feet before he gave in to temptation and kissed Lilah, Zane examined the lantern, which still contained an oily swill of kerosene.

He found a plastic lighter in the rucksack and tried to light it. Frustratingly, the lighter wouldn't ignite. On closer inspection he discovered that the cheap firing mechanism had broken. Tossing the lighter back in the rucksack, he tried the old brass lighter, which had to date back before World War II. It fired instantly. Seconds later, the warm glow of the lantern lit up the cave. "Close on seventy years old and it still works. They should keep making stuff like this."

Zane caught the quick flash of Lilah's smile, and held his breath at the way it lit up her face, taking her from pale and gorgeous to high-voltage, sexily gorgeous.

She held his gaze with a boldness that took him by surprise and made his heart race then looked quickly away, her cheeks pink.

She shrugged. "Sometimes I forget you're an Atraeus."

He shrugged, his jaw clenched in an effort to control the sudden hot tension that gripped him, the desire to compound his sins by grabbing her and kissing her until she melted against him. He had to keep reminding himself he was trying for a measured, adult approach, in line with his desire to try an actual relationship. "Before I was an Atraeus I was a

Salvatore. In L.A. that meant pretty much the opposite of what Atraeus means on Medinos."

"And that's when you got the scars?"

He found himself smiling grimly. "That's right. Pre-Spiros."

Picking up the lantern, he held it high. "Wait here. I'm going to check out the rest of the cavern."

And take a few minutes to regain the legendary Atraeus control that, lately, was losing hands down to the hotheaded Salvatore kid he used to be.

When he returned, Lilah was on her feet. Automatically, he set the lantern down and steadied her, his hands at her waist.

She released the rock shelf she'd grabbed and clutched at his shoulders. "Every time I see you lately, I seem to lose my balance."

"I'm not complaining."

With a calm deliberation formulated during a sleepless night and several hours out on the water, he eased a half step closer, encouraging her to lean more heavily on him. "That's better."

She wound her arms around his neck with an automatic, natural grace that filled him with relief. Despite the disastrous conversation the previous night, she still wanted him.

Her breasts flattened against his chest, sending another jolt of sensual heat through him, but he couldn't lose his cool. He had said that the next time they made love they were going to go about it in a rational, adult way, and he was sticking to that.

Lilah met his gaze squarely. "Why did you sail away on your own?"

A chilly gust of wind laced with rain swept into the cave.

"I wanted to give you time to think things through. If you had wanted off the island that badly, I would have taken you, but—"

"I don't."

His mouth went dry at her capitulation. A split second later thunder crashed directly overhead.

Lilah lifted a brow.

"Come and see what I found." An uncomplicated satisfaction flowed through Zane as he picked up the lantern and helped Lilah through to the rear part of the cavern, which narrowed and curved then widened out to form a second room.

The cavern was furnished with a table and two chairs, a small antique dresser and a chaise longue. As dusty and faded as the furniture was, the overall effect was elegant and dramatic, like a set for an old Valentino movie.

"What is this place?"

Zane set Lilah down on one of the chairs and stripped what proved to be a dustcover off the chaise longue revealing red velvet upholstery. "I'd guess we've found the location of Sebastien Ambrosi's love nest."

Lilah touched the velvet. She had heard the tale from her grandmother, who had known Sebastien quite well. According to Ambrosi family history Sebastien had asked for Sophie Atraeus's hand, but in order to save the then failing Atraeus finances, Sophie had been engaged to a wealthy Egyptian businessman. "Where he was supposed to meet with his lover, Sophie Atraeus."

"You know your history."

Zane's gaze was focused and intent as he pulled pins out of her hair. Heart pounding, she clutched at his sleek shoulders. With slow deliberation, his mouth settled on hers. Automatically, she lifted up on her good foot and wound her arms around his neck.

The kiss was firm, but restrained. After a night of tortured wrestling with her values, all undermined by a fevered anticipation that had kept her from sleeping, it was not what she had expected.

Wry amusement glinted in his eyes. "I'm trying to slow things down a little."

"Under the circumstances, it's a little late to worry about being PC."

His hands closed on her hips, pulling her in close against him. "Is that un-PC enough for you?"

She buried her face against his throat, breathing in his scent, reassured by his tentativeness, charmed by his consideration and the touches of humor. "What are you afraid of? That you might lose control and we'll end up having unprotected sex?"

He reached into his pocket. Moments later he pressed a foil packet into her hand. "That won't happen again."

Suddenly the murky afternoon was hot and airless.

His mouth captured hers again, this time frankly hungry. She felt the hot glide of his palms on her chilled skin as he peeled the damp camisole up her rib cage. Obligingly, she lifted her arms so he could dispose of the garment altogether. Moments later her bra was gone.

She braced herself against his shoulders as he unfastened her shorts and peeled them along with her panties down her legs.

When he straightened, she unfastened and unzipped his jeans. He assisted by toeing off his trainers and stepping out of damp, tight denim.

Lacing her fingers with his, he pulled her close. Heat flooded her at the intimacy of skin on skin.

The sound of the wind increased, damp air stirred through the cavern, raising gooseflesh on her skin. Zane wrapped her close. "This is no place to make love."

She buried her face in the muscled curve of shoulder and neck and breathed in his scent. "It was good enough for Sebastien and Sophie."

"Almost seventy years ago." He cupped her nape and fastened his teeth gently on the lobe of one ear, sending a bolt of heat clear through her. "I was thinking modern-day bed, silk sheets, soft music."

"Where's your sense of adventure?"

"Back in L.A.," he said drily.

Releasing her, he pulled her down with him onto the chaise

longue, their legs tangling, the weight of him shatteringly intimate. The chaise longue was narrow and unexpectedly hard, but the discomfort was instantly forgotten as the heat of his body swamped her.

She kissed him, wanting him with a fierceness that shook her. She could feel the heat and shape of him against her inner thigh and remembered the foil packet, which she was still holding. "I might need some help with this."

His teeth gleamed. He relieved her of the condom. "Leave it to me."

With expert movements, he sheathed himself, reminding her that while she was a novice, Zane operated at the other end of the scale. His experience and conquests were legendary. Seconds later, he moved between her legs. She felt the hot pressure of him, a moment of shaky vulnerability at what she was allowing, then the aching rush of pleasure.

For long seconds she couldn't think, couldn't breathe. Zane simply held himself inside her, his gaze locked with hers. And endless moment later he began to move. Not hurried and edged by anxiety, but a slow, tender rhythm that squeezed her chest tight, gathered her whole being. Lovemaking as opposed to the stormy few seconds they had shared in Sydney.

Zane's gaze locked with hers as sensation drew them together, swept her in dizzying waves, shoving her over an invisible precipice as the coiled intensity shattered.

For long minutes Lilah floated, disconnected and content, happy to wallow in the intimacy of Zane's solid weight, the heart-pounding knowledge that there was much more to lovemaking than she had ever imagined.

As if he'd read her thoughts, he lifted his head and braced himself on one elbow. He framed her face with his free hand, stroking his thumb across her bottom lip. "Next time, we're making love in a bed."

Twelve

The vibration of Zane's cell broke the warm contentment.

He extracted his phone from his jeans and checked the screen. "Sorry. Work call. The downside of a satellite connection." Pulling on his jeans, he walked out into the first part of the cavern to take the call.

Cold now that Zane was gone, Lilah found her damp clothes and quickly dressed. The squall had passed and watery sunshine filtered into the cave, relieving the oppressive gloom.

Curious about the meeting place of the two lovers who apparently had been forbidden to see each other, she studied the room. When Sophie had disappeared during a bombing raid during the war, it was rumored that Sebastien had taken her with him to Australia. Sebastien had denied the claim. The unresolved questions had been a bone of contention between the two families ever since.

Lilah opened a cupboard in the dresser and found a small wooden box and a letter. The box contained a missing set of bridal jewels that she instantly recognized. She had designed jewelry based on Sebastien's sketches of this very set. They had belonged to the Atraeus family, and Sebastien had been blamed for stealing them.

Heart speeding up, she extracted a piece of fragile, yellowed paper. She could read a little Medinian, better than she could speak it, enough to know she was looking at a love letter.

Zane strolled in, sliding the phone into his jeans pocket. She showed him the jewels then handed him the letter.

"Sophie Atraeus's final love letter to Sebastien Ambrosi." He set the letter down beside the casket of jewels. "Well, that solves the mystery. Sophie boarded one of the ships that sank with all hands. She was lost at sea."

"And she left the bridal jewels here."

"Probably for safekeeping. When the islands were evacuated, a lot of families hid their valuables in caves. To Sophie it would have made perfect sense."

Lilah touched her fingertips to a delicate filigree necklace. "These are more than jewels, they're history. And a record of love."

Zane's dark, assessing gaze rested on her.

Feeling faintly embarrassed, she closed the box and tested her weight on her sore ankle. "I think I can walk now."

Zane took the box from her, set it down on the table and drew her close. "Not yet. Later."

By the time they left the cave, the storm had cleared and it was twilight. A slow walk down the hillside, heavily assisted by Zane, and they reached the house on sunset. The fairy-tale quality of the afternoon extended into the evening with another candlelit dinner beneath the stars.

The tension of the previous night seemed a distant memory as the dishes were cleared away. When Zane pulled back her chair and linked his fingers with hers, it seemed the most natural thing in the world to go to bed together.

When Lilah woke the next morning, she was alone. Feeling disappointed, because she had looked forward to waking up with Zane, she quickly showered and dressed in a white halterneck top and muslin skirt. When she walked out onto the deck, still limping slightly, Zane was seated at the table, drinking coffee and answering emails.

Zane got to his feet and held her chair. "Your ankle's still swollen."

"Only a little. The stiffness should wear off while I walk." Feeling let down that he hadn't kissed her, but reasoning that Zane was probably distracted by whatever work situation he was dealing with, she sat and poured herself a glass of freshly squeezed orange juice.

"You won't need to walk much." Zane bent down and kissed her on the mouth.

The warm pressure, the sudden intensity of his gaze, broke her tension. The dire suspicion implanted by a number of women's magazine articles, that now they had made love and she was a "sure thing" Zane was losing interest, receded.

Zane checked his watch as he returned to his seat. "We're going back to Medinos. I've called in a ride.

By ride, Zane had meant the Atraeus family's private helicopter. Concerned about her ankle and despite her objections, Zane insisted she should get it checked out by a doctor. The helicopter set them down in the grounds of the Castello Atraeus. Zane transferred their luggage to his car and drove her to a private clinic located in downtown Medinos.

They were greeted by a plump and cheerful doctor. A few minutes later they were back out on the street. Lilah, now almost free of the irritating limp, walked as briskly as she could toward the car.

Now that they were back on Medinos, she was aware that as wonderful and earth-shattering as her time with Zane was, it had to be over. She couldn't afford to abandon her arrangements just because Zane wanted to be with her for a few days.

Zane insisted on helping her into the passenger-side seat then slid behind the wheel with a masculine grace she doggedly ignored. She would have to get used to viewing him as one of her bosses again, although with the sleek width of his shoulders almost brushing hers and the hot scent of his skin it was going to be difficult.

"Okay," he said flatly. "What's wrong?"

Lilah ignored the flash of irritation in his eyes and tried to focus on her happy place, which at present was the bland fence that encircled the parking lot. "Nothing. I need some processing time."

He actually had the gall to pinch the bridge of his nose as if he was under extreme stress. "This would be a feminine thing."

Her gaze clashed with his and the fact that she had not only made love with Zane *a number of times* but was actually considering canceling the series of blind dates she had set up for next week, for him, hit her forcibly.

She stared at the masculine planes of his face, the narrowed eyes and tough jaw, the moment of disorientation growing.

He was too wealthy, too attractive and too used to getting exactly what he wanted. The wild fling had been a mistake. She must have been out of her mind thinking that she could ever control any part of a relationship with Zane. "We've had the two days, it has to be over."

His brows jerked together. "We could spend a few more days together. I know you have vacation time coming up, but you don't fly back to Sydney until the end of next week."

She felt her brain scramble. "An affair wasn't on my priority list. I have things to do—"

"Like checking out online marriage prospects."

There was a ringing silence. "I don't know how you knew that, but yes."

"Stay with me until the end of the week." He started the engine and put the car in gear.

Her chest squeezed tight as he turned on to the spectacular coast road with its curvy white-sand beaches and sea views. After which time she would seldom see Zane, if at all, because he worked mostly in the States.

"Talk to me, Lilah."

She turned her head, which was a mistake, because Zane's gaze was neither cool nor distant, but contained a flash of vulnerability that tugged at her heart. For a split second she was filled with the dizzying knowledge that Zane truly wanted to be with her. "I don't know that it's a good idea to continue."

Lilah's fingers clenched on her handbag. The last thing she had expected was that Zane, with his freewheeling approach to love, would try to keep her with him, even if only for a few days.

She should hold firm and finish it now. Staying with Zane could wreck her plans for the secure marriage she needed. She was already distinctly unmotivated at the thought of meeting the men in her file.

But it was also a fact that since she had undertaken the search for a husband a great many things had changed; *she* had changed.

She was now financially secure and no longer based in Sydney. The financial pressure of her mother's mortgage was gone.

She was no longer a virgin.

The difference that made was unexpectedly huge. She now knew that if she was not passionately attached to her prospective husband, she would not be able to go through with the physical side of the relationship.

She was aware that this restriction would drastically reduce her chances of finding someone. She was almost certain that none of the men on her list would fulfill her new requirement, but she was no longer worried. She could marry, or not. It was her choice.

The sense of freedom that came with that thought was huge.

She still wanted a stable marriage, but she no longer felt she *had* to marry in order to be happy or secure. Now she had a much more important goal: she wanted to be loved.

Zane turned into the drive that led to the Atraeus Resort and pulled in under the elegant portico.

Lilah signed the register then followed Zane to the bank of elevators. "What if I say 'no' to more time together?" The instant the question was out she knew it was a fatal mistake.

Elevator doors slid open.

Zane gestured that she precede him. "I'm counting on the fact that, when it comes to us, you don't have a big track record with 'no.'"

The abrupt switch to teasing charm, and Zane's use of the word *us* threw her even more off balance. "A gentleman wouldn't say that."

He hit the button to close the door. "But then, as we both know, I'm no gentleman."

No. He was mad and bad and dangerous to know. He had turned her life upside down, and he was still doing it.

Almost a whole week with Zane before she committed herself fully to the tricky business of finding a husband. The thought was dizzying, tempting.

She couldn't say no.

"All right," she said huskily. "Six more days."

"And then it's over."

She tensed, stung by the neutrality of his tone, the implication that he would be relieved when the affair came to an end. "You make it sound like the resolution to a problem." One of his troubleshooting projects.

Zane bent his head and brushed her mouth with his. "It is a problem, and it has been for two years."

Six days.

She no longer wanted to concentrate on the men she had planned to meet and date next week. But neither could she afford to abandon her series of interviews altogether.

Zane was not abandoning his life for her. She still needed to plan for the future. She would need something to hold on to when he had gone.

The doors of the elevator opened. Lilah stepped out into the expensively carpeted corridor of the penthouse level. Zane opened the door to a suite.

Decorated in subtle champagne-and-pink hues with elegantly swagged curtains, the suite was both gorgeous and spacious. A glass coffee table held a display of lush pink roses, tropical fruits, a plate of handmade chocolates and an ice bucket with champagne and two flutes.

There were two bedrooms.

Lilah was aware of Zane talking to a bellhop who had delivered their luggage.

While Zane tipped the bellhop she continued to check out the rooms.

Except for the colors, the suite was a mirror image of the one they had shared in Sydney. The separate bedrooms contained identical four-poster beds swathed in diaphanous champagne silk and gorgeous en suite bathrooms. Everything was carefully arranged so that two people could live separate lives in the same suite.

She sensed his presence behind her a split second before she heard the sound of her case being placed on the stand just inside the door. She caught Zane's reflection in a large ornate mirror and her heart turned over in her chest.

When she turned, one broad shoulder was braced against the door frame. He had brought just the one suitcase, she noted, hers. She realized he had already placed his case in the other bedroom.

She set her handbag down on the end of the bed. "This is a two-bedroom suite."

His gaze was neutral. "I prefer to sleep alone."

Her stomach and her heart plunged.

Desperate for a distraction, Lilah switched her gaze to her cases. "Oh good, you've brought my laptop."

She forced a bright, professional smile and grabbed the lifeline of an internet connection.

"You're going to work?"

Blinking back a sudden urge to cry, she picked up the computer case. "I have some private correspondence to see to."

Blindly, she walked past Zane out into the sitting room

and headed in the direction of an elegant writing desk. Placing the case on the glass-topped surface, she busied herself setting up the laptop.

Zane's clinical approach to their sleeping arrangements, his rejection of any depth of intimacy, was a reminder she badly needed. Now more than ever, she needed to carry through with her schedule for the following week.

Zane frowned as he watched Lilah. The blank look in her eyes tugged at him, warring with his habit of carefully preserving his emotional distance. He was almost certain she was crying.

Instead of backing off, he found himself irresistibly drawn as she booted up her computer. "I thought we could go out for lunch."

"That sounds nice."

Zane frowned at the brisk note in Lilah's voice. He glanced at her laptop screen. The separate rooms dilemma suddenly evaporated. "Are these online 'friends' all male?"

"As it so happens, yes."

The emotional calm he had worked so hard to maintain since the riveting hours in the cave was abruptly replaced by the same fierce, unreasoning jealousy he had experienced when he had found out that Lucas was taking Lilah to Constantine's wedding. "Have you dated any of them?"

She fished spectacles out of her handbag, pushed them onto the bridge of her nose and leaned a little closer to the screen as if what she was reading was of the utmost importance. "Not yet."

Dragging his gaze from the fascinating sight of the spectacles perched on the delicate bridge of Lilah's nose, he studied the list of men she was perusing. The lineup of photographs portrayed a selection of Greek gods, some flashing golden tans and overly white teeth, some dressed with *GQ* perfection. The one exception was a slightly battered, bleach blond surfer type.

Lilah scrolled and he glimpsed the logo of the matchmaking agency. The lightbulb flared a little brighter. "But you intend to?"

"That's right. Next week when I have my annual vacation."

His gaze snagged on the four men who had withdrawn. He noted the dates. Just days after the scandal had erupted into the newspapers.

He also noted that the flood of new applications had all come in at a similar time. "How many?"

"Fifteen so far." She scrolled down to a chat page, which had several comments posted. "Seventeen if two other very good prospects come on board."

The corporate-speak momentarily distracted him. He had to remind himself that the businesslike approach was entirely consistent with Lilah's view of marriage. She didn't just want a man, she wanted a paragon, someone who would tick every one of the boxes on her corporate marriage sheet.

Someone who possessed all of the steady, reliable qualities that he clearly did not. "This is why we only have a week. You're fitting me in before you go back to Sydney to find a husband."

Her gaze remained glued to the screen. "If I'm seeing someone from the agency I can't be involved."

Involved. He suddenly knew the meaning of stress.

Lilah could feel Zane's displeasure as he studied the emails pouring into her mailbox.

Abruptly, she found herself spun around in her chair. Irritation snapped in his gaze and she realized she had pushed him too far with the list.

"Is that all this is?"

She dragged her spectacles off. "You said it yourself. Marriage doesn't come into our equation."

"I thought we had an agreement."

"We do, but long-term commitment is the one thing I do want. The reason I haven't been able to settle on anyone is because you've always been in the picture just often enough to blot out any other prospects."

The expression in his gaze was suddenly remote. "Are you saying I'm responsible for your decision to advertise for a husband?"

"No." *Yes.* She stared at the screen and tried to pinpoint what had driven her to such an extreme. It had been after the last charity auction, she realized. Zane had been there with Gemma.

Lilah had spent an entire agonizing evening trying not to be aware of Zane and failing. Afterward, she had decided she needed to deal with the fixation by making plans for the future. It had been a relief to come up with a workable plan.

It was not a good time, she realized, to acknowledge that her approach had been naive and too simplistic. The strength of her plan had relied on the screening process of a matchmaking company and the integrity of the men who had replied, which was a fatal flaw. With her family history, she should have known better. "I've tried normal dating. This seemed a more...controllable option."

Grimly, Zane decided that he shouldn't be pleased he had effectively blotted out the other men in Lilah's life. Neither should he be annoyed that Lilah dismissed him as secure relationship material, when that was the stance he had always maintained.

He should be more concerned with distancing himself. Given that they only had six days left to douse the fatal attraction that threatened to ruin both of their lives, it was not a good time to feel fiercely possessive.

Emotionally, he did not get involved; he had learned the hard way that love had conditions. It literally took him years to trust anyone, and he could count those he did trust on one hand.

That ingrained wariness of people made him good at his job. He didn't take anything for granted. His approach was often perceived as clinical and heartless. Zane didn't bring emotion into the process; he simply did the job he was paid to do.

But somehow, despite his background and his mind-set, he *was* involved. "Just what do you think every one of those guys who answered your ad wants?"

"A steady, stable relationship."

"Do you believe in the tooth fairy?"

"This is not a good time to be sarcastic."

"Then don't believe in this. It's not real."

He straightened and stabbed a finger at one of the photos of a bronzed, sculpted torso. The handsome, chiseled face rang a bell. He couldn't be sure, but he had a suspicion it belonged to a male model, probably from some underwear billboard. "*They* are not real."

"Which is exactly why I intend to conduct one-on-one interviews next week. If they're not genuine, I'll know."

There was a moment of vibrating silence. "This is the reason you have to be back in Sydney?"

"Yes."

"Where, exactly, do you intend to conduct these interviews?"

"At restaurants and cafes. They're not interviews exactly. More a series of…blind dates. After I conduct online interviews to screen candidates."

Blind dates. Suddenly Zane needed some air.

Thirteen

Pacing to a set of French doors, he jerked them open, although he was more interested in Lilah's reflection in one of the panes than the sun-washed balcony. "Did you give them your real name?"

"Yes. And a photograph."

"Along with your occupation." Lilah was nothing if not thorough. His tension ratcheted up another notch. "When the recent publicity hit the newspapers, they would all have instantly recognized you."

Lilah could feel herself going cold inside. Of course she had considered that angle, but she had been guilty of hoping that the original list of five steady, reliable men she had assembled would be too sensible to read the gutter press, or to connect the wild stories with her resume.

Zane's gaze, reflected in the glass, was neutral enough to make her feel distinctly uncomfortable. "The whole point of the exercise is marriage. What did you expect me to do? Pretend to be someone I wasn't?"

"Like the guys who replied."

Her gaze was inescapably drawn to a couple of the photos, which she suspected were of male models and not the candidates. In the case of one particularly stunning man, she was almost certain she had seen him on an underwear billboard. "I'm well aware that some of the applications are not honest."

There was a vibrating silence. "I have resources. If you want I can have them screened by the private investigative firm The Atraeus Group uses in Sydney."

For long seconds she wavered, but given the media exposure that had made her temporarily notorious, she couldn't afford not to have Zane's help. He was in the business of checking and double-checking on the integrity of businesses and personnel. She did everything she could to research the candidates, but with limited time and resources, she couldn't hope to do any in-depth checking in the span of a few days. "Okay."

Lilah brought up her file of applicants and vacated the chair. Zane sat down and began to scroll through, the silence growing progressively deeper and more charged as he read. "Do you mind if I email the file to my laptop?"

"Go ahead."

Seconds later, he exited her mail program and rose from the chair. "I'm going to have these names checked out. The firm I use has access to criminal files and credit records. I'll order lunch in, it shouldn't take more than a couple of hours to get some basic details back." An hour and a half later, Lilah stared at the list of men on her dating site, her stomach churning at the thought of what Zane could turn up. While she had waited for the results of his investigation, she had eaten one of the selection of salads that had been delivered by room service then made herself coffee in the small kitchenette.

She sipped the coffee, barely tasting it. Six days together. She blinked back a wave of unexpectedly intense emotion. It wouldn't be six days of making love; it would be six days of saying goodbye.

Jaw set, she forced her attention back to her laptop screen and began reading through all of the mail. She had expected to have a few withdrawals—what she hadn't expected was for four of her five vetted men to have quit her page and the raft of new applications.

A prickling sense of unease hit her. She had compiled her previous list of stable, steady men over months from the un-enthusiastic trickle of replies to her dating agency application. In the span of two days she had lost four of the five steady prospects she had intended to meet the following week and had received fifteen new "expressions of interest." Not good.

She scrolled through the emails, flinching at some of the subject lines.

Clearly, it had been an easy matter to connect the scandal-ous stories in the press with her matchmaking page. Most of her solid prospects had quit and she was now being targeted by men attracted by her notoriety.

Zane strolled into the suite. "A handful of the applicants checked out." He tossed a pile of papers down on the desk. "Don't reply to any of these. If you do, you can count on my presence at any interviews you conduct because, honey, I'll be there."

Lilah swallowed the impulse to argue a point she was in one hundred percent agreement with herself. She did not want to end up at the mercy of some kind of kinky opportunist or worse, a reporter trying to generate another smutty story. "I don't see how. You won't be in Sydney next week."

Zane strolled toward his bedroom, unbuttoning his shirt and shrugging out of it as he walked. "For this, I'll make a point of it."

Lilah dragged her gaze from Zane's broad back, and the unsettling, undermining intimacy of watching him undress. With an effort of will, she squashed the impulse to walk up be-hind him, wrap her arms around his waist, lean into his heady warmth and breathe in the scent of his skin. "I don't see why when you made it clear you don't want anything more than a temporary arrange—"

"You want more than the one week time limit?"

Lilah tried to squash the heart pounding thought that they could extend their affair for weeks, maybe months. The reason she was keeping the time so short was to get the fixation with Zane out of her system. She couldn't in all honesty enter into a marriage with someone else if she was still attracted to Zane.

Although, she was already certain she had made a fundamental mistake. The desperate fixation *had* faded somewhat, but it had been replaced with something much more insidious.

She was beginning to *like* Zane. Neither her mother nor her grandmother had ever mentioned liking their lovers. There had simply been the dangerously out-of-control passion, which had been dispensed with when the pregnancies had become apparent.

She avoided answering him and instead stared at the papers Zane had tossed down on the desk. On the top was the underwear ad guy. In reality, he was a forty-five-year-old, twice-divorced mechanic who had somehow managed to make his application from a minimum-security prison cell.

According to the detective firm Zane had employed, he was currently serving a two-year sentence for car theft. With time out for good behavior, he could be out in six months.

The sound of running water in Zane's shower broke the heavy silence that seemed to have settled around her. She skimmed the information on the rest of the applicants Zane had blacklisted. Logging back on to the matchmaking site, she deleted them from her page. That left her with six applicants in total, one from her previous batch of applicants, and five new ones. Three were depressingly unsuitable, so she deleted them. That left her with three.

The sound of the shower stopped.

She tried to concentrate on the photos and profiles of the three remaining men on her dating list. Jack, Jeremy and John, the three J's.

They were all pleasant, attractive men in solid jobs. John Smith, wearing a crisp, dark suit, looked like an ad for *Gentleman's Quarterly*. Listed as the CEO of his own company, he fitted the profile she had put together for a husband perfectly.

The one applicant who had not deserted her following the scandal in the newspaper, Jack Riordan, had been high on her list. He wasn't perfect, but it was heartening that her top pick apart from Howard, who had not worked out, was still on board.

Taking a deep breath she decided she needed to reward Jack Riordan's loyalty for sticking with her despite the scandal, take the plunge and commit to an initial date.

She typed in a suggested meeting time and place and hit the return key. Her computer made a small whooshing sound as the reply was sent. A split second later her message appeared on her page.

Stomach tight, pulse hammering, she stared at the neat print. After months of lurking online, reluctant to commit to anything more than a little window-shopping, she felt she was finally moving forward with her plans. She ought to feel positive that, while she wouldn't have Zane in her life, at least she had the possibility of having *someone*.

There were no strings, she reminded herself. Half an hour in a coffee shop or over a lunch table, and if she didn't like Jack, or vice versa, they need never contact one another again.

The thought was soothing. On impulse she quickly typed in affirmatives for the other two men. Now more than ever, with the end of her time with Zane set and the knowledge that hurt was looming, it was important to stay focused.

She stared at the three messages on screen and her stomach did a crazy flip-flop. The decision shouldn't feel like a betrayal of Zane, but suddenly, very palpably, it did.

With a jerky movement, she pushed back from the desk, rose from her seat and strolled to the French doors. She stared out at the serene view of sea and the distant, floating shape of Ambrus.

A shiver went through her as she remembered the hours spent making love to Zane on Ambrus, then further back to the stormy interlude in Sydney.

Unhappy with the direction of her thoughts, she walked through to the bedroom and began to unpack. Long seconds ticked by as she emptied her suitcase and tidied it away in a large closet.

Despite trying to put a positive spin on the process of finding a husband, every part of her suddenly recoiled from the idea of replacing Zane in her life.

In her bed.

She walked back out into the sitting room and began to pace, too upset to settle. Her stomach was churning; she actually felt physically sick. She had the sudden wild urge to erase the messages she had sent, because she knew with sudden conviction that no matter how wonderful or perfect any one of the three J's might be she was no longer sure she was ready to offer any of them a relationship. The thought of sharing the same intimacies with another man that she had shared with Zane made her recoil. She couldn't do it.

The truth sank in with the same kind of absolute clarity she experienced when she knew a painting was finished or a jewelry design was completed. It was a complication she should have foreseen. She had tried to get Zane out of her system, but she had done the exact opposite of what she had planned to do. She had fallen wildly, irrevocably in love with him.

In retrospect, the damage had been done two years ago when she had first met him at the charity art auction.

She wondered why she hadn't seen it from the first. Clearly she had been so intent on burying her head in the sand and denying the attraction that she had failed to recognize that it was already too late.

She had been a victim of the *coup de foudre*. Struck down somewhere between the first intense eye contact when she had strolled into the ballroom that night over two years ago and the passionate interlude at the end of the evening.

With her history she should have sensed it, should have *known*. Her only excuse was that neither her mother nor her grandmother had ever mentioned a lingering fascination or liking coming into the equation. Cole women were notoriously strong-willed. As soon as the pregnancies, and their lovers' unwillingness to commit, had become apparent, the relationships had ended.

If she'd had any sense, as soon as she had registered the unusual power of the attraction she would have gotten as far away from Zane Atraeus as she could. Instead, she had offered to donate more paintings to his charity, gotten involved with fundraising, even volunteered to help with the annual art auctions. Every step she had taken had ensured further contact with Zane.

It was no wonder she had not been able to let go of the fixation. In her heart of hearts that was the last thing she had wanted. She had hung around him like a love-struck teenager, secretly sketching and painting him.

She had compounded the problem by legitimizing the affair as an exercise to get Zane out of her system. Instead she had succeeded in establishing him even more firmly in her life, to the extent that now she didn't want anyone else.

She had been in love with Zane for two years. There was no telling how long she would remain in love, but given the stubborn streak in her personality, it could be for years. Quite possibly a *lifetime*.

She still wanted a stable marriage and a happy family life. She wanted love and security and babies, the whole deal. But she no longer wanted them with some unknown mystery man in her future.

She wanted them with Zane.

Zane strolled out as she headed back to the desk, dressed in a soft white shirt and a pair of faded, glove-soft jeans.

Aware that the screen of her laptop portrayed the appointments she had made, and which she was now desperate to retract, Lilah made a beeline for the desk.

Zane, who clearly had the same destination in mind, reached her laptop a split second before she did.

The scents of soap and clean skin and the subtle, devastating undertone of cologne made her stomach clench.

Zane touched the mouse pad. The screen saver flickered out of existence, revealing the three postings she had made.

To Lilah's relief there were no replies, yet. In Sydney it would be midmorning. All three J's would be at work.

"You've made times to meet." Zane's voice was soft and flat.

Lilah stiffened at his remoteness; it was not the reaction she had expected. The lack of annoyance, or even irritation, that she was progressing with her marriage plans was subtly depressing.

With the suddenness of a thunderbolt his cool neutrality settled into riveting context. She had seen him like this only once before, when he had been dealing with a former treasurer of the charity who had "borrowed" several thousands of dollars to pay for an overseas trip. Zane had been deceptively quiet and low-key, but there had been nothing either soft or weak about his approach. Potter had taken something that mattered to Zane, and he wasn't prepared to be lenient.

Zane had quietly stated that if the money wasn't back in the account and Potter's resignation on his desk by the end of the day, charges would be laid and Zane would personally pay for and oversee the litigation.

Potter had paled and stammered an apology. He hadn't been able to write the check fast enough.

Lilah had always been aware of Zane's reputation for taking no prisoners in the business world. The element that had struck her most forcibly was that the charity had mattered to him *personally*.

Hope dawned. She knew she mattered to Zane; he had admitted as much. As hard as she had struggled to stay away from him, he had struggled to stay away from her, and failed.

Because she mattered to him on a level he could not dismiss.

By his own admission, he had become more involved with the charity than he had planned because she was there. They had ended up together on Medinos and in Sydney. They'd had unprotected sex. For a man who was intent on staying clear of entanglements, that in itself was an admission.

Then there was the small matter of Zane virtually kidnapping her for two days.

She felt like a sleeper just waking up. She had been so involved in the minutiae of day-to-day events and her own plans for marriage that she had failed to step back and look at the bigger picture.

Zane cared for her. He said he cared about who she was with next. Although it was a blunt fact that Zane did not have a good track record with helping her to find love. He had gotten rid of Howard and a raft of dating applicants. He had effectively made sure that Lucas remained in her past.

There was only one conclusion to be drawn: Zane was jealous.

The tension that gripped Lilah eased somewhat as possibilities she hadn't considered opened up, expanded.

If Zane was jealous, then maybe, just maybe, there was a chance that he could overcome his phobia about intimate relationships and commit to her.

The possibility condensed into a breathtaking idea.

Relationships were not her strong area; hence the marriage plan. It had not been successful, but at least it had given her a framework—a system—to move forward with, and that was what she needed with Zane.

Not a marriage plan. The stakes were suddenly dizzyingly, impossibly high. She needed a strategy to encourage Zane to fall in love with her.

It was a leap across a fairly wide abyss, but in that moment of realization she had already mentally taken that leap. The future stretched out before her in dazzling, Technicolor brilliance. Not just a steady, reliable marriage, but one based on true love.

Once Zane fell for her, she was confident the whole marriage thing would take care of itself. There was a risk involved, but when Zane succumbed to love, the intensity of the emotion should be powerful enough to dissolve whatever objections he had to marriage.

Heart pounding, Lilah stared at the incriminating dates on the screen. It occurred to her that the proposed dates had a positive angle. They could generate the pressure that was needed to convince Zane that he couldn't bear to let her go.

The about-face in thinking was a little disorienting but she was already adjusting to the new direction. The sudden itch to sit down with a pad and pen and start formulating a plan was the clincher.

She could do this.

She had no choice.

She would begin by waiting a day or so before she canceled with the three J's. Taking a deep breath, she smiled pleasantly and answered Zane's question. "I didn't see much point in waiting around."

Zane's brows jerked together. "There's every point. You should have waited for the in-depth security checks."

Lilah's mood soared at his bad temper. "You didn't mention a further check. In any case, other than the very thorough checks you've already conducted there's nothing more that can be done unless you intend to put them under twenty-four-hour surveillance—"

She was caught and held by the complete absence of expression on Zane's face. "That is what you were planning on doing, isn't it?"

Zane's gaze met hers for a searing moment. "Yes."

The small, delighted shock wave she felt at his admission was replaced by a sudden breathless anticipation as he studied the screen. Lilah felt like a kid at Christmas, waiting to unwrap a gift. The surveillance only proved her point. It was the kind of extreme thing one did when they were falling in love.

The discovery made her feel like dancing a jig around the sunny room. She had clung to the depressing view that Zane was elusive and superficial and absolutely not good husband material. Now wasn't a good time to feel that, despite all the areas they did not fit, crazily, he was perfect for her.

Zane stabbed a key and began studying profiles. "You've chosen Appleby, Riordan and Smith. I wouldn't trust Smith. His first name's John—that makes him close to invisible in terms of security information."

Lilah kept her expression smooth and professional. "The initial dates, are just a meet and greet, they do not imply commitment."

There was a vibrating silence, broken by the near silent sound of an indrawn breath. With controlled movements, Zane picked up the hotel folder, which lay next to her laptop and flipped to the page of restaurant listings as if food was suddenly paramount. "You could withdraw from the process."

The barely veiled command in his voice made her want to fling her arms around his neck and hug him. To prevent herself from looking deliriously happy, she picked up a pen and pad and started working on her new plan of action by making an important note. She could not afford any over-the-top displays of affection until Zane capitulated. She allowed her brows to crease, as if she had just remembered that Zane had said something but was too distracted to recall his exact words. "Why should I do that?"

Zane, who seemed more interested in the restaurant he was choosing than their conversation, picked up the sleek phone on the desk, although his grasp on the phone was gratifyingly white-knuckled. "Given the recent publicity, I'm not inclined to trust any of the three. If you won't accept surveillance reports then I'm going to have to insist on being present at the interviews."

Lilah tapped her pen on the notepad. "Let me get this right.

You don't want a relationship with me, yet you'll take time off to make sure I'm…"

"*Safe* is the word you're looking for."

Lilah was momentarily sidetracked by the stormy look in Zane's eyes. A quiver of anticipation zinged down her spine then she registered Zane's emphasis of the protection angle. She was certain he was using it as a handy excuse to avoid admitting to anything else. "You can't come to the interviews."

She had no problem being firm on that point since she intended to cancel all three dates. "What would I tell the applicants?"

Zane froze in the act of dialing the hotel restaurant. "Tell them you're no longer available."

Fourteen

Zane allowed the singular truth that he was burningly, primitively possessive of Lilah to settle in.

With a sense of incredulity, he realized that he had made the kind of rash, male, territorial move he had only ever observed in other men.

He had crossed a line and now there was no going back.

He eased his grip on the phone and set it back on its rest a little more loudly than he had intended.

Lilah, who was in the process of shutting down her computer, was oddly composed. There was a distinct air of expectation that made his jaw compress.

She closed the laptop with a gentle click. "What exactly do you mean by 'no longer available'?"

Her gaze was carefully blank, but he detected the hopeful gleam in her eye. He knew with utter certainty that she wanted him to say marriage.

Bleak satisfaction that he had finally made it on to Lilah's list of marriage candidates was tempered with irritation that it had taken so long, and the old, ingrained wariness. He could feel the jaws of Lilah's feminine trap poised to snap shut.

As much as he wanted Lilah, he would not be maneuvered into a relationship that would leave him vulnerable. Years had passed since his mother had abandoned him, not once, but a number of times in pursuit of well-heeled lovers or husbands. He would never forget how it had felt to have the rug pulled out emotionally, to be relegated to last place on her list when he had needed to be first. By the time his father, Lorenzo, had found him at age fourteen, he'd had difficulty forming any relationships at all.

Remembering the past was like staring into a dark abyss. The level of trust involved in committing to any kind of intimate relationship still made him go cold inside. The progress he had made over the past few years was monumental but he was not capable of moving any further forward with Lilah now unless he could be absolutely, categorically certain of her love.

Unfortunately, Lilah's continued focus on finding a steady, reliable husband suggested that he was not even close to being number one in her life.

Grimly, he realized that part of his wariness revolved around the certainty that, because of his shadowy past and inner scars, a breakup was inevitable. And when it happened, *he* would most likely be the instigator of the betrayals.

"What exactly do you mean by 'no longer available'?"

Grimly, he examined Lilah's question, and the demand that had surprised them both.

Unlocking his jaw, he answered her question. "I think we should try...living together."

"For how long?"

Zane, arrested by Lilah's calm response, watched as she strolled to the kitchenette and extracted a bottle of water from the fridge. He had the sudden, inescapable feeling that he had ventured into a maze and was being herded by a master strategist.

To his surprise he found there was an element of relief to

the thought that Lilah would try to ruthlessly manipulate him into an even deeper commitment. He had always viewed her methodical approach to getting what she wanted from relationships as calculating. Now, it occurred to him that with his past he could not afford to go into a relationship with a woman who was too weak or too frightened to try to hold on to him. "I don't know."

She poured a glass of water and walked sedately in the direction of the bedroom. "Let me think about it."

The door to her bedroom closed quietly behind her.

Zane stared at the closed door for long seconds.

His heart was pounding, his jaw locked. He was aware that Lilah had just pulled off a feat that no one in either his professional or his personal life had attempted in a good ten years.

She had put him on hold.

She had kept her three agency dates, with him on the side.

For the first time since he was a teenager on the streets he experienced what it felt like to be shut out, although the feeling was somewhat…different.

As a teenager, he had been running on survival skills and desperation. That was not the case now. In his job as the Atraeus Group's troubleshooter, he had spent years dealing with people who were intent on closing doors in his face.

Probably the most important skill his father had taught him was that when it came to negotiating there was always a way. He either found another door or he made his own, whatever got the job done.

It was an odd moment to realize that his time as a homeless kid had created qualities in him that had uniquely fitted him out for problem solving. For one thing, he did not give up easily. He was also used to operating from a losing position, and winning.

Something in him cleared, healed.

He was aware of a sense of lightening. He was no longer fourteen and at the mercy of forces and people he could not control. Ten years on, he had a certain set of life skills and a considerable amount of money. Those two factors provided him with an edge that had been formidably successful in business.

A sense of relief filled him. In the business arena he had never been defeated no matter how unpromising the situation. He did not see why he couldn't apply the same strategies that had been so successful in business to a relationship. The only wonder of it was that he had never thought of that before.

His decision made, he strolled to his computer and found the details the security firm had supplied for the three men Lilah had chosen.

Strolling into the kitchenette, Zane opened the fridge. It was depressingly empty. He had missed lunch and his stomach felt hollow and empty. Now hungry as well as frustrated, he pulled out a beer and called down to room service for a pizza.

He walked back to his computer, intending to catch up on some correspondence. On the way, he noticed that Lilah had forgotten to take the bridal-white leather-bound folder with her.

The last time he had seen the contents of the folder had been when Lilah had dropped it on the floor of the jet on her first flight out to Medinos. He had only read snatches; just enough to understand that it contained the kind of inside information that would be very useful to him right now.

The sound of the shower in Lilah's en suite bathroom was the decider. The phrase "all is fair in love and war" took on a new resonance as he picked up the folder and carried it out to the terrace to read.

Setting the beer on the table, Zane pulled out a chair, sat down and began flipping through the pages. There was a formatted set of profiles, complete with photographs, a series of neatly handwritten notes including underlined notations highlighting domestic prowess, and a punitive points system.

A failed marriage carried a penalty of ten points. The total any one man could earn was twenty. Divorce wasn't complete disaster, but close.

That was one blot that couldn't be entered against his name, however his sense of gratification evaporated when he read the next line. Serial dating was penalized almost as heavily, carrying a maximum demerit of eight.

The scoring range from four to eight indicated there was room for movement in that category depending on the seriousness of the misdemeanor.

There was a zero tolerance for fathering an illegitimate child. Immediate disqualification was indicated.

The list went on, including a number of ways in which points could be earned. Gifts were good; a maximum of five points could be redeemed. The scoring wasn't based on the value of the item, which could be as simple as a flower. Apparently, the ability to *personally* select gifts was key. Jewelry was a time-honored indicator because it spoke to emotional value. Significant jewelry was a sign about how the rest of the relationship would go.

He had just taken the last swallow of beer when his gaze snagged on the last item on the demerit list. A penchant for junk food and beer indicated a lack of nutritional responsibility that could carry over into Other Areas.

Directly below the demerit list, typed in boldface so it couldn't be missed, was a notation: three strikes and you're out.

His fist closed on the now-empty beer can. Absently, he placed the crushed aluminum on the patio table. From inside he heard a knock on the door. Room service, no doubt, with the pizza he had ordered.

He paid the young waiter, added a generous tip and told him to give the pizza to a family with young kids he had noticed staying farther down the hall. Somewhere between demerit items eight and nine, his appetite had faded.

The shower was still running, so he walked back out to the patio, got rid of the beer can in the kitchen trash then sat down and flipped through to the end of the folder. There were a number of rejected profiles at the back. Lucas and Howard were the most recent additions to that section.

The final sheet was a list of discarded Possibles: men who Lilah knew through business and social connections or the dating website, but who had not made it through to the selection process.

Snapping the folder closed, Zane replaced it on the table and paced to the terrace railing. Gripping the wrought iron edge, he stared out at the stunning view of the bay.

The contents of the folder had given him an insight into what Lilah wanted from a man. However, the most significant fact from his point of view was that *he* did not even make it into the folder.

Lilah had not even considered him in her discarded possibles list.

Jaw tight, he strode back to the table and flipped through to the points system. He was aware of his shortcomings, but he did not think he was that bad. It annoyed him that Lilah had not even considered him as a possible.

As if all he was good for was a quick thrill.

He found the merit list and the notation he wanted: number five, gifts.

A visual of the large solitaire ring Lucas had gotten Elena to order from an online store flashed into his mind. Lucas's instincts had been good, although he had fallen down with his inability to personally select the ring.

Flipping back to Lucas's rejected profile, he noted that Lucas had not scored in the gifts area. Somehow he had managed to amass *nineteen* points without presenting Lilah with any kind of gift.

Bleakly, he wondered what Lucas had done with the ring he had bought. If it fell into Carla's hands, Lucas would have some fast talking to do.

Not that Zane was interested in obtaining the solitaire, or anything like it.

He had a better idea.

* * *

Lilah had expected dinner in the hotel restaurant to be a little tense after she had left Zane strategically hanging. However, instead of the frustration she had glimpsed that afternoon, Zane seemed relaxed and oddly preoccupied, as if his mind was on other things.

Twice he had taken calls on his cell, getting up from the candlelit patio table to pace around the enormous floodlit infinity pool, looking taut and edgy in black pants and a loose black shirt.

To make matters worse, Gemma, who Lilah had thought was based in Sydney, was seated at a nearby table. According to Zane, his former P.A. had just transferred to a position on Medinos, and now worked for the manager of the resort. She started her new job at the end of the week.

Looking young and sexy in a minuscule hot orange dress that should have clashed with her titian hair but somehow didn't, Gemma succeeded in making Lilah feel staid and old-fashioned in the classic white silk sheath she had chosen.

Every time Lilah's gaze was drawn to Gemma, the weight of every one of her twenty-nine years seemed to press in on her. Gemma looked far more Zane's type than she could ever be. It was a depressing fact that in the dating game, classic Hepburn just did not cut it with Lolita. Her sexuality had finally been released, but it was clear that if she wanted to keep Zane's eyes on her, she was going to have to update her wardrobe.

She stared bleakly at the exquisite table arrangement of pink roses. Panic gripped her at the thought that she *had* overplayed her hand. That instead of giving their relationship a discreet nudge toward marriage, she had pushed too hard and Zane was now cooling off.

Zane finished his call and returned to the table. Their dessert, an island specialty he had insisted on ordering, was delivered with a flourish. Lilah tried to show an interest in the exquisite platter of almond pastries and sweetmeats sprinkled with rose petals, but she had lost her appetite.

A wine waiter materialized beside the table with a bottle of very expensive French champagne. As if they had something to celebrate.

Candlelight, roses, champagne, all the classic elements of a grand romantic gesture.

The depression that had settled on her like a dark shroud dissipated, wiped out by a sudden dizzying sense of anticipation. Her heart began to pound. She felt like she was on an emotional roller coaster ride. Her instincts were probably all wrong, but she couldn't blot out the sudden, wild notion that Zane was about to propose.

Zane leaned forward and the subtle but heady scent of his skin and the devastating cologne made her head swim. "Do you see anything you like?"

Her gaze was caught and held by the piercing quality of his eyes. In the candlelight his irises were midnight dark with an intriguing velvety quality. He frowned and she realized he wanted her to look at the dessert that had just been delivered.

She surveyed the dessert tray. Almost instantly, she saw the glitter of jewels in the center.

Her excitement evaporated. Not an engagement ring; a diamond bracelet.

The standard currency for mistresses.

At that moment, Gemma, who was leaving with her escort, stopped at their table.

Her gaze moved from the discreet pop of the champagne cork to the bracelet. She smiled brightly. "Diamonds." She waggled one slim, tanned wrist, displaying a narrow gold bangle that shimmered with tiny stones. "Doesn't Zane give the *best* presents?"

While the waiter poured flutes of champagne, Gemma lingered, introducing her date. She eventually left in a flurry of lace ruffles and floral perfume.

Zane handed Lilah a flute of champagne, which she noted

was pink, to match the rose petals. She tried to be upbeat about that fact. Zane had gone to a great deal of effort to create a special occasion, and he had brought her a gift, which was significant.

Unfortunately, somewhere between discovering the bracelet and the conversation with Gemma, the sizzle of excitement had gone.

His gaze held a hint of impatience. "Do you like it?"

Lilah set the champagne down without tasting it. Grandma Cole had gotten a diamond bracelet from her lover, shortly before he had left her. She had used it as a down payment on a small cottage for her and the baby.

Reluctantly, she extracted the bracelet from its nest of confectionary and petals. It was unexpectedly heavy for such a delicately, intricately constructed piece. Her breath caught as she noted the cut and the quality of the emeralds interspersed between the diamonds. Not new, but old. Make that *very* old.

She frowned. The design was hauntingly familiar. She was certain she had seen something like it before, although, in the flickering light of the candles, she couldn't be sure. Curiosity briefly overrode her disappointment as she studied the archaic design.

She itched to put her spectacles on and examine the bracelet more closely, but she couldn't afford either the professional or the emotional attachment. Not when it looked like a bracelet was Zane's standard form of dating gift.

Despite all of the reasons she could not accept the bracelet, a small part of her didn't want to relinquish it. The value of the stones didn't come into it. The bracelet could have been made of plastic. What mattered was that Zane had thought to give her a gift, a keepsake of their time together.

Unfortunately, old or new, she couldn't risk accepting the bracelet in case Zane took that as her tacit agreement to a relationship with him on his terms.

As his temporary live-in lover.

After the way he had interfered with her dating program

that afternoon, she knew that if she weakened, Zane would be relentless.

Reluctantly, she placed the bracelet on the table.

Zane frowned. "Aren't you going to try it on?"

"It's lovely, but I can't accept it."

"If this is about Gemma, you don't have to worry. She was my personal assistant, nothing more."

"I don't think she sees it that way." Gemma's attitude toward Zane had always been distinctly proprietorial. So much so that for most of the past two years, Lilah had thought she *was* Zane's steady girl.

He looked impatient. "Which is why she isn't my P.A. anymore. The bracelet was a goodbye gift."

Lilah made an effort to calm emotions that were rapidly spiraling out of control. She had to keep reminding herself that she was with Zane now, not Gemma. "Goodbye, and she transfers to Medinos?"

It would not have been the way she would have handled the situation.

"I couldn't fire her, and she liked Medinos. It was a solution."

Lilah's fingers clenched. Gemma had clearly gotten emotionally involved and Zane had found a way of shifting her out of his work space, while still letting her have her way and stay close.

And think that she still had a chance.

It was a perfect example of Zane's nice side. From her dealings with him in the charity, Lilah knew he didn't like seeing anyone in a vulnerable situation get hurt. He would go out of his way to personally help. She loved that evidence of his compassion but she couldn't help wishing that Zane had been a bit more ruthless with Gemma.

Another unsettling thought occurred to her. If Zane had not given Gemma a definite "no" she had to wonder how many other discarded women still lingered on the fringes of his life in the hope that a relationship was still possible.

It was not a happy thought. Zane was nothing like the irresponsible, self-centered men who had abandoned her mother and grandmother, nevertheless the scenario with Gemma was unsettling in a way she hadn't quite worked out.

Ignoring the champagne and the dessert, Lilah got briskly to her feet.

Now visibly annoyed, Zane slipped the bracelet into his pocket and rose to his feet. He fell into step with her as she threaded her way between the tables, easily keeping pace.

His palm cupped her elbow, sending tingling heat up her arm. His gaze locked on hers. "Why won't you accept the gift?"

Lilah ignored the gritty demand and the pleasure that flooded her that, finally, Zane was responding in the way she had hoped. She focused on a bland section of beige wall in an effort to control the wimpy desire to give in, fling her arms around his neck and melt against him. "It's...too expensive."

"I'm rich. Money is no object."

They emerged from the restaurant. A little desperately she eyed the bank of elevators ahead. "It's not about the value, exactly."

Zane released her elbow as they reached the elevators. She caught a flash of his expression in the glossy steel doors. He looked disbelieving and grimly annoyed.

"Do I get points for trying?"

Her gaze snapped to his. "You *read* my folder."

"I needed to see what I was up against."

Lilah jabbed the elevator button. A door slid open. "That would be commitment."

After a night of passion that was curiously unsatisfying, Lilah rose early and spent time alone, adapting elements of the marriage plan to suit the new strategy. She decided the best way to show Zane that she was not fretting over the way their brief fling, apart from the heart-pounding sex, seemed to be disintegrating was to throw herself into her work.

During the early hours, she had given herself a pep talk

about the positives. Zane had responded to her elusiveness with a gift. It had been the wrong gift and he had cheated by reading her folder, which was a blot. She was prepared to overlook his behavior on the basis that he had not thought things through. The one shining factor was that he had made his choices based on the desire to win her. It was progress.

For the next two days she got up early and walked to Ambrosi's new retail center, a charming, antiquated building situated on the bustling waterfront. Interior decorating wasn't her job, but the retail center would be her temporary office until the facility on Ambrus was completed. Lilah figured that if she had to work there for the next six months she needed to like her surroundings, so she pulled rank and inserted herself into the process.

Zane, who had had to spend long hours closeted with Elena working through the raft of paperwork on a deal in Florida, had become even more remote. Despite their lovemaking, the abyss between them seemed to be widening.

With her strategy seemingly in tatters, it was hard to concentrate on paint colors and curtain samples when all she wanted to do was take a taxi back to the resort and throw herself into Zane's arms.

To avoid weakening, she had taken herself shopping during the long, somnolent lunch breaks the Medinians enjoyed. Instead of eating, she had spent a large amount of money on filmy, sexy clothes and a daring hot orange bikini that she gloomily decided she would probably never get the opportunity to wear.

New makeup that made her eyes look smoky and exotic, subtle caramel streaks in her hair and a fake tan completed the makeover. Every time she caught her reflection in glass doors or looked in a mirror, Lilah was amazed at the difference the subtle changes had made, although Zane had barely seemed to notice.

Tempted as she was to bluntly declare that she was in love with him and put an end to the tension, Lilah made a grim effort to appear sunnily content. She couldn't shake off the dreadful conviction that the instant Zane knew she had fallen for him, he would put an end to any hope of long-term commitment.

That was how it had worked with her mother and her grandmother. Once the prize was won, the passion had cooled. Their lovers hadn't been able to leave fast enough.

Zane strolled into the building chaos just short of noon. Wearing dark narrow trousers and a loose white shirt, sunlight slanting across his taut cheekbones, he managed to look both dangerously sexy and casual.

Lilah was instantly aware of her own attire. Instead of her usual low-key neutrals, today she was wearing one of her new purchases, a filmy orange blouse teamed with a tight little black camisole that revealed just a hint of cleavage and tight, white jeans. Combined with strappy orange heels and iridescent orange nail polish, the effect was unexpectedly striking.

Zane's gaze glittered over her. Lilah registered the gratifying flare of shock that was almost instantly shuttered.

Zane had finally noticed her. Although, it could simply be the orange color, which she had developed something of a fetish for lately. Orange was hard to miss.

Just minutes ago she had felt warm, but comfortable. Now, beneath the weight of Zane's gaze, despite all of the doors and windows flung wide admitting the balmy sea breeze, Lilah felt flushed and overheated.

"Are you ready to go?"

That afternoon Zane had planned a boat trip to survey Ambrosi's old oyster beds and the site for the new processing plant. The trip would be followed up by a launch function for the new enterprise at the castello.

Lilah ignored the faint edge to Zane's voice and kept her attention on Mario, the builder. She had spent the morning directing a number of contractors as they had fitted air-conditioning and lighting fixtures and erected partitioning. Mario was a little on the short side, but outrageously handsome. On a purely intellectual level she had thought she should feel something for such a good-looking man. Depressingly, the only thing she had felt had been the battle of wills as Mario had tried to improve on her floor plan. "Almost."

Zane's gaze shifted to the bronzed contractor who was hefting a dividing panel into place. Mario had already repositioned the panel for her twice. Both times the angle had not been quite right. As a consequence he was sweating, his T-shirt clinging damply to his chest.

Mario placed the partition and finally got it right. She rewarded him with a smile. "*Bene*."

Zane's fingers interlaced with hers. A split second later she found herself pulled into a light clinch. Her heart pounded as Zane's gaze settled on her mouth. The move was masculine and dominant and, in front of the contractors, definitely territorial.

His mouth brushed over hers, sending a hot pulse of adrenaline through her. It was a claiming kiss, the kind of reaction she had wanted two days ago.

Two days. Panic made her tense. Time was sliding away, only four days left. Suddenly, it didn't seem nearly enough time for Zane to fall in love with her.

Zane's hands settled at her waist, making her feel even hotter. This close she could see the nicks of long-ago scars, the faint kink in a nose that should have been perfectly straight, the silky shadow of his lashes. She drew in a breath and just for a few seconds, gave herself permission to relax.

Zane cocked his head to one side. "Is this a 'yes'?"

She stiffened at the lethal combination of pressure and charm. "Yes, to the boat trip."

The midday sun struck down, glaringly hot on the marina jetty, as Lilah walked on ahead while Zane unloaded dive gear from the trunk of the car. She rummaged in her new string beach bag for a pair of dark glasses as she strolled, drawn by the bobbing yachts and the aquamarine clarity of the sea.

Movement on Zane's yacht drew her gaze. The bleached

surfer hair on one of the men rang an instant alarm bell, although neither of the other two men on the yacht were remotely recognizable.

Although, if it was the three J's she was looking at, she shouldn't be surprised. If most of the applicants had been scammers, the odds were not good for the three she had picked.

Suddenly any idea that Zane had been suffering the agonies of an emotional crisis for the past two days was swept away. The entire time she had been playing her waiting game, he had been busy working on a preemptive move.

By the time Zane appeared, stripped down to a pair of sleek black neoprene dive pants, his chest bare, a gear bag filled with diving equipment, there was no doubt.

Jaw set, she met his gaze. "How did you get them here? Wait, let me guess—Spiros."

What was the point in having a henchman unless he could do useful things like kidnap all three of her potential husbands?

Fifteen

The lenses of Zane's dark glasses made him look frustratingly remote and detached. "You make it sound like Spiros kidnapped them. All he did was pilot the jet."

That was like saying that all Blackbeard did was sail the ship. "How did you get them?"

The idea that they had been coerced in any way evaporated as she took in their collective grins, the clink of beers. A definite holiday air pervaded the yacht. "No wait, don't tell me, it was a corporate kidnap." She slid her dark glasses onto the bridge of her nose. "Two days. *Paradise*."

Zane shrugged. "They could have refused."

"Hah!"

His gaze narrowed. "If you don't want to spend time with them just say the word. Spiros can take them out for the afternoon, no problem."

Which was, she realized, exactly what he wanted. He hadn't brought the men here so she could get together with them. His plan was much simpler than that. He was intent on ruthlessly cutting them out of her life.

She squashed the thrill that shot through her at his un-PC behavior and jabbed a finger in the direction of his chest. "You had no right—"

He caught her hand and drew her close, his hold gentle as he pressed her palm against his bare chest. "While you're with me, I have every right. I told you I wanted to be present when you met them."

Lilah's toes curled at the fiery heat of his skin against her palm, the thud of his heart, the sneaky, undermining way he had gotten around the issue of crashing her dates. "I didn't agree."

Although, she realized that none of that mattered now, because it was clear Zane had never considered any of the men as serious contenders. If he had, he would not have brought them to Medinos.

She stared at the obdurate line of his jaw. In a moment of blinding clarity, she recognized the flip side of the situation, an even more important truth. Zane wanted her enough to eliminate the three J's in the first place. Far from ignoring her for the past two days, Zane had been focusing his energies on systematically clearing away all opposition so he could have what he wanted. As if her agreement to his proposition was a forgone conclusion.

He jerked his head in the direction of the yacht. "It's your choice. If you don't want to spend time with them, you don't have to."

Tension hummed through her along with an undermining, utterly female sense of satisfaction. It was difficult to stay mad at Zane for completely subverting her strategy when a part of her adored it that he had gone to such lengths to cut out the competition.

He wanted her, enough that he couldn't bear the thought of her having other men in the picture. It was exactly the result she had wanted; it just hadn't panned out the way she had thought.

A dazzling idea momentarily blotted out everything else. She was suddenly glad for the concealment of the dark glasses. "Not a problem," she said smoothly.

Mentally, she ticked off a number of new, exciting options all based around having three extra men in close proximity for the afternoon. "Now that they're here, why not meet them?"

Seconds later, Zane handed Lilah onto the yacht.

Jack Riordan, clearly an outdoors kind of guy and at home on the yacht in a pair of board shorts and a tank, looked exactly like his photo. Jeremy Appleby did not. Instead of tall and dark, he was blond and thin, with a goatee. He also had an impressive camera slung around his neck, which put Lilah on instant alert.

Zane's gaze touched on hers. The knowledge that he had also noted the camera formed a moment of intimacy that sent pleasure humming through her. Despite everything that was wrong between them, in that moment she felt utterly connected to Zane, as if they were a couple.

She also felt protected. Next to Zane's and Spiros's tanned, muscular frames, Appleby looked weak and weedy. Lilah would not want to be in Appleby's shoes if he tried to take photos or file a story.

Like Appleby, John Smith did not look anything like the *GQ* photograph he had supplied. With his plump build, balding head and glasses, he didn't come close.

A blond head popped out of the cabin, breaking the stilted conversation. Lilah recognized the pretty flight attendant from the jet. Though she was dressed now in a bright pink bikini teamed with a pair of low-slung white shorts, evidently Jasmine was fulfilling the same role, because she had a tray of cold drinks.

Lilah noticed that Jack Riordan seemed riveted by Jasmine's honey-blond hair and mentally crossed him off her now-defunct list.

After casting off, Spiros took the wheel. To Lilah's relief, Zane didn't leave her alone with the three men, but stayed glued to her side. Her relief was short-lived as Zane systematically questioned each of the three J's about their lives, concentrating on their finances.

An hour into an agonizingly slow trip, which bore more of a resemblance to the Spanish Inquisition than a pleasure cruise, they reached Ambrus.

Zane dropped anchor. Spiros heaved the inflatable raft into the water, preparatory to rowing to the beach. The three J's trooped below to change into their beachwear.

Lilah clamped down on her frustration and helped Jasmine take glasses and bottles to the galley. When she emerged on deck, Zane was securing the inflatable. She checked that the three J's were still below. "You had no right to interrogate them like that."

Apart from the fact that it had been embarrassing, it had utterly nixed any opportunities to make Zane jealous. She had barely been able to get a word in edgewise.

Zane knotted the rope to a cleat and straightened. "Did you really believe Appleby owned his own software company?"

When he had not seemed to know the difference between a megabyte and a gigabyte, it hadn't seemed likely. "No."

"Or that John Smith is the CEO of an accounting firm?"

She had not caught on to all of the jargon Zane, who had a double degree in business administration and accounting, had dropped into the conversation, but she had understood enough to know that John Smith had failed the test. "Jack Riordan seems genuine." His knowledge of the yacht at least seemed to back up his small boat-building business.

At that moment, the three men emerged on deck, ready to board the inflatable. Appleby and Smith, their alabaster skin slathered with sunblock, appeared to glow beneath the brassy Mediterranean sun.

If Lilah had been fooled, even for a second, that Zane was

doing this out of the kindness of his heart, that notion would have now been completely discredited.

First the inquisition, now the swimsuit contest.

When they reached the beach, Jasmine tossed her shorts on the sand, laid out a bright yellow towel and lay down to sunbathe. While Zane and Spiros assembled snorkeling gear, Lilah strolled behind a clump of shade trees to change. Setting her beach bag down on the sand, she extracted the hot orange bikini, which she had been reluctant to change into on the yacht.

Before her courage deserted her altogether, she quickly changed then knotted the turquoise sarong that went with the bikini around her hips. She frowned at the lush display of tanned cleavage and considered changing back into her white jeans, camisole and shirt.

Even as the thought passed through her mind she knew she could not afford to do that now. She had lost the leverage of the three J's and she was almost out of time. Unfortunately, the bikini was now a crucial part of her strategy.

Zane almost had a heart attack when Lilah emerged onto the beach. He was glad Spiros had taken the three J's on a snorkeling expedition. It was an easier solution than the medieval threats he would have been forced to issue just in case any one of them decided it was okay to look.

The cut of the outrageously sexy bikini somehow managed to make Lilah's narrow hips and delicate curves look mouthwateringly voluptuous. Added to that, after just a few days on Medinos, her skin had taken on a tawny glow that made her green eyes look startlingly light, her cheekbones even more exotic. In the span of a few minutes, Lilah had gone from mysterious and reserved to lusciously, searingly hot.

If she had bought the bikini for the specific purpose of driving him crazy, Zane thought grimly, she had achieved the result. "When did you get the bikini?"

Lilah, who seemed more interested in laying out a bright turquoise towel and rummaging through her trendily match-

It was not a new concept. It was Zane's modus operandi with relationships. The fact that she could not make Zane fall in love with her was the basis that had undermined her entire strategy. "It's a common enough scenario. Women fall for you on a regular basis."

Irritation registered in his gaze. "I get partnered with women on a regular basis through company business and charitable events. That's mostly what the tabloids pick up on. The only woman I know who has certifiably fallen for me is you."

The knife twisted a little deeper. "And that makes me a sure bet."

His hands curled around her upper arms, his palms shiveringly hot against her skin. "You were a virgin, and you've got a logical, methodical approach to relationships. That's what I trust."

Jaw set, Lilah resisted the gentle pressure to step closer to Zane. She would not muddy this process any further with passion. They had already been that route. And what Zane proposed was sounding more like a business deal than a relationship.

The vibration of his cell phone broke the taut silence.

Frowning, Zane released his grip and checked the screen. He looked briefly frustrated. "I have to go. There's something I need to take care of before the official part of the evening begins."

Lilah strolled back to the party and circulated, chatting with buyers and contractors. She checked her wristwatch. Long minutes had passed since Zane had excused himself.

She walked out on the terrace just in case he had come back and she had somehow missed him. The terrace was windswept and empty.

She strolled back inside and surveyed the reception room again. Zane was not in the room.

It suddenly occurred to her that neither was Gemma, and with her flaming red hair and white skin, the younger woman was unmistakable.

The last time she had seen Gemma, she had been heading toward the part of the castello where the private suites were located, and suddenly she knew what the desperate look she had sent Zane had meant.

Feeling like an automaton, Lilah stepped out of the reception room. A ridiculously short amount of time later she found herself in the castello's darkened hallway, the chill from the thick stone walls seeping through the silk of her red gown.

She paused at the door of Zane's private quarters and lifted her hand to knock. The chink of glass on glass signaled that the suite was occupied.

A grim sense of déjà vu gripped her. She rapped once, twice.

It occurred to her that this time, unlike the incident with Lucas, Zane could not rescue her because, in a sense, she was confronting an aspect of herself that she did not like very much.

The door swung open on a waft of perfume. Gemma's tousled red hair cascaded around her white shoulders. Slim fingers clutched a silky black negligee closed over her breasts, the defensive gesture making her look young and absurdly vulnerable.

Lilah couldn't help thinking that it looked like they had both had the same idea about setting the scene for seduction.

She felt the weight of every one of her twenty-nine years crushing down on her. Her irritation with Gemma evaporated. "You should stop trying and go home. Sex won't make Zane, or any man, have a relationship with you."

"How can you know that?"

Because it had been burned into her psyche by both her mother and her grandmother. Unfortunately, she had temporarily forgotten that fact. "Logic. If you couldn't make him fall in love with you in two years, then it's probably not going to happen."

Gemma's expression went blank, as if she didn't know what to say next.

A split second later, the door snapped shut in Lilah's face.

Lilah fumbled the key into the lock of her door and let herself in. The door closed with a soft click behind her.

She stared at the glowing lamp-lit room, the sexy, filmy negligee draped over the bed.

The preparations were wrenchingly similar to Gemma's, and the end result would be the same. She could not make Zane love her, either.

She had changed, through falling in love with him, but she had to accept that for Zane the past might never be healed.

Feeling numb and faintly sick, she jammed the negligee out of sight in the case, picked up the phone and made a quick call to the airport. She managed to secure a flight to Dubai, which was leaving in an hour. She would have several hours to wait before she could get a connection to Sydney, but that didn't matter. She could leave Medinos tonight.

She arranged for a taxi then changed into clothes suitable for a long flight—cotton pants and a sleek-fitting tank, a light jacket and comfortable shoes. She caught a glimpse of the red crystal earrings dangling from her lobes in the dresser mirror as she packed. She removed them with fingers that were stiff and clumsy, wound her hair into a knot and secured it with pins.

She did a final check of the room then tensed when she realized she was lingering in the hope that Zane would come looking for her.

Swallowing against the sudden pain squeezing her chest, she walked down to the lobby of the castello. She didn't have time to stop at the hotel and collect all of her things. That would have to wait until she returned to Medinos at the end of her vacation.

Not a problem.

By the time she came back, Zane, who was involved in a set of sensitive negotiations in the States, would probably be gone. The retail outlet would be almost ready to open and construction of the pearl facility on Ambrus would be underway.

She would be busy interviewing and training staff. In theory she wouldn't have time to think.

When she reached the forecourt the taxi pulled into a space. A chilly breeze blew off the ocean, whipping strands of loose hair around her cheeks as she climbed into the backseat. She checked her wristwatch. Time was tight, but she would make her flight.

Her throat closed as the taxi shot away from the castello. She was still reeling from the speed with which she had made the decision to leave, but she could not have done anything else.

She was not a "glass half full" kind of girl and now she was in love.

Until Zane, she hadn't been even remotely tempted to break her rule of celibacy. It would have taken a bolt of lightning—literally a *coup de foudre*—to jolt her out of her mindset, and that was what had happened. She had seen Zane and in that moment she had lost her bearings. She had committed herself emotionally and now she didn't know how to undo that.

She could not accept the marriage agreement he had been clearly working toward. She refused to die a lingering emotional death, like Gemma.

She stared bleakly ahead, at the taxi's headlights piercing the dark winding ribbon of road.

There was no going back. It was over.

Seventeen

Zane knocked on Lilah's door. When there was no answer, he walked inside. A quick inventory informed him that she had packed and left.

He strode to his suite. Any idea that Lilah had made an executive decision and moved in with him died an instant death. The moment he opened the door and caught the scent of Gemma's signature perfume, his stomach hollowed out and he understood exactly what had gone wrong.

A split second later, Gemma emerged from his bedroom, fully dressed, but the filmy negligee clutched in one hand told the story.

Suppressing the raw panic that gripped him, he strode past Gemma and found his wallet and his overnight bag. "How long ago was Lilah here?"

Gemma watched from the safety of the sitting room as he flung belongings into the bag. "Fifteen minutes." She stuffed the negligee into her evening bag and sent him an embarrassed look. "You don't have to worry, I won't do this again."

Zane zipped the bag closed and walked to the door. He couldn't be angry with Gemma, not when he was responsible for this mess. He had been guilty of the same sin Lucas had committed when he had tried to keep Carla at a distance. Now his strategy had backfired on him. "Good. You should keep dating that guy you were with the other night. He's in love with you."

"How do you know?"

Zane sent her a stark look.

Gemma blinked. "Oh."

He waited pointedly at the door for Gemma to leave. He knew the boyfriend was somewhere downstairs, because Spiros had run a standard security check on him before the invitation to the castello was issued.

Once Gemma was gone, he headed for the front entrance.

He resisted the urge to check his watch. Lilah had been gone a good fifteen minutes. It only took ten minutes, max, to get a taxi out to the castello.

He reached the forecourt in time to see the red taillights of a taxi disappearing down the drive. There had been a lone occupant in the rear seat.

Constantine's aide, Tomas, who was greeting late guests, confirmed that the occupant had been Lilah.

Zane strode to the garage, found his car and accelerated after the taxi.

The repercussions of Gemma's stunt kept compounding. He hadn't touched her, but with his past and his reputation, no one, least of all Lilah, would believe him.

He reached their hotel suite and walked quickly through the rooms, long enough to ascertain that Lilah was not there, nor had she returned. That meant she had gone straight to the airport.

Using his cell, Zane checked on flights as he took the elevator down to the lobby. There was an international departure scheduled in just under an hour. He made a second call. The Atraeus Group owned a significant block of shares in the airport itself. Enough to ensure that when Zane needed assistance it was never a problem.

He reached the airport in record time and strode to the airline desk. As he spoke to the ticketing officer, his fingers automatically closed around the small jewelry case he had retrieved from the family vault before he had discovered that Lilah had left.

She loved him. He could hardly believe it.

And all he had been prepared to offer her was a loveless marriage, a business deal that would allow him to stay safe emotionally.

In retrospect the offer had been cowardly, a cover-up for his own failings and a situation he would not have been able to sustain, since a business arrangement was the last thing he wanted from Lilah.

His chest felt tight, his heart was pounding. For years he had been focused on the betrayals in his past. After all of *his* betrayals of Lilah, he was very much afraid that he had finally lost her.

The boarding call for Lilah's flight was announced as she strolled toward the gate. Buttoning her jacket against the air-conditioned chill, she joined the line of passengers.

A male voice with an American accent sent hope surging through her. She checked over her shoulder. For a split second she thought she saw Zane then she realized the man was shorter, darker.

Until that moment, she hadn't realized how badly she had wanted Zane to come after her.

Blinking back a pulse of raw misery, she kept her gaze pinned on the flight board, which was now showing a "delayed" message, and shuffled forward. She dug her boarding pass out of her purse as she neared the counter.

Behind her there was a stir. The deep register of another masculine voice that sounded even more like Zane made her tense. Determinedly, she ignored it.

Someone said "Excuse *me,*" in an offended tone.

Her head jerked around, her gaze clashed with Zane's.

His eyes were dark and intense, his expression taut. "I didn't touch her."

A hot pulse of adrenaline that he *had* come for her momentarily froze her in place. "I know."

He looked baffled. His hand closed on her elbow.

Despite the fact that her heart was pounding so fast she was having trouble breathing, Lilah gently disengaged from his hold. She knew how this worked. Once Zane got her out of the line he would start taking charge and she would melt; she would have trouble saying "No."

"She wasn't there at my invitation and there never was a 'me and Gemma.' She was only ever a…convenient date."

Lilah blinked, then suddenly she knew. "For the charity functions."

Zane's gaze was level. "That's right."

She suddenly felt short of air. "If you felt you needed protection from me, why did you even bother to come?"

"The same reason I'm here now. I couldn't stay away."

An announcement came over the speaker system that the flight was delayed. Lilah made another heart-pounding connection. "*You* delayed the flight."

"Being a member of the Atraeus family has its uses."

Lilah dragged her gaze from the sexy five o'clock shadow on his jaw and tried to concentrate on the bright hibiscus-printed sundress of the woman ahead of her. "Why did you have the flight delayed?"

The woman wearing the flowered dress gave her a fascinated look.

Zane's dark gaze held hers with a soft intensity. "Because there's an important question I need to ask you."

Panic gripped her, because hope had flared back to life and she couldn't bear it if he presented her with another variation of a loveless marriage.

Boarding resumed. "I have to go and you can't come with me."

He held up his boarding pass.

There was a smattering of applause.

Lilah dragged her gaze from the grim purpose in Zane's eyes. So, okay, he could board the flight, she couldn't stop that. "What did you want to talk about?"

"It's uh—private."

A nudge in the small of her back from the passenger behind prompted her to move forward another step. She was only feet from the counter now, but boarding the jet had ceased to be a priority. Every part of her being was focused on Zane, but she was afraid to read too much into his words. "I can't accept a temporary relationship. I still need what I've always needed—commitment."

His brows jerked together. "I'm capable of commitment. Don't believe everything the tabloids print. I've dated, but since I met you there hasn't been...anyone."

For a fractured moment the ground seemed to tilt and shift beneath her. She was certain she had misheard. "Are you saying you haven't slept with *anyone?*"

He frowned, his gaze oddly defensive. "It's not unknown for men to be celibate."

Heads turned. There was a visible stirring in the gate area. Somewhere a camera flashed.

Lilah's stomach churned. Just their luck, there was a journalist in the queue.

Zane's arm curved around her waist. "Is the fact that I was celibate so hard to believe?"

Still stunned by the admission, Lilah didn't protest when he hustled her out into the relative privacy of the corridor. "No. *Yes.*"

The thought that he hadn't wanted to be with another woman since he had met her was dizzying, terrifying.

"I don't lie."

Her mouth went dry. It explained why he had lost control in Sydney. Despite her resolve to stay distant and cool, she was riveted by the thought. "What I don't get is, with all the women you could have, why me?"

Zane sent her a frustrated, ruffled look as if he was all at sea. "You're sexy, gorgeous. We have a lot in common with the business, art, our pasts. I like you. I *want* you."

Her heart squeezed in her chest. Liking and wanting, not *loving*.

He drew a velvet box from his pocket and extracted a ring.

The jewelry designer in her fell in love with the antique confection of diamonds and emeralds. The ring was heart-breakingly perfect.

And he wanted to marry her.

Lilah swallowed against the powerful desire to cave and say yes. "You chose a ring you knew I couldn't resist."

"I'll do what I have to, to get you."

Her jaw tightened at the neutral blankness of his approach. "What if I say, no?"

"Then I'll keep asking."

Once again the neutrality of his tone hit her like a fist in the chest then suddenly she saw him, suddenly she *knew*.

At age thirteen, he would have used that tone on the streets: with the gang that had cornered him and beat him; with the police and welfare workers who had shifted him from place to place; with his mother when she had finally decided to come looking for him.

It wasn't that he didn't care. It was because he did.

The strain of his expression, the paleness of the skin beneath his tan registered as he gripped her left hand, lifted it, the movements clumsy.

Raw emotion flooded her when she saw the unguarded expression in his eyes. When she didn't withdraw from his grip the flash of relief almost made her cry.

He slid the ring onto the third finger. The fit was perfect.

Lilah stared at the glitter of diamonds, the clear deep green of the emeralds, the ancient, timeless setting. But mostly what she saw was the extreme risk Zane had just taken with a heart that had been battered and bruised, and for a few years, lost.

Somewhere in the recesses of her mind, she registered that the ring he had slipped onto her finger was a part of the priceless Illium Cache of jewels that his buccaneering ancestor had once claimed as booty.

The ring matched the bracelet he had tried to give her.

She swallowed. He had been trying to tell her then.

According to the material she had read tonight the cache was a bridal set; there had always been a ring to match the bracelet. More than that, they were heirlooms: family jewels.

As a jewelry designer she knew the message of the gems themselves was purity, eternity. Love.

She met Zane's gaze and the softness there made her heart swell. "This belongs in your family."

"Which is exactly where it's staying, if you'll marry me." For a moment he looked fiercely, heartbreakingly like his ancestor.

His fingers threaded with hers, pulled her close. "I wanted to give it to you before the opening ceremony tonight. That's why I had to leave when I did. Constantine has the combination to the vault, which is down in the cellar."

He had wanted her to wear the ring in front of his family and all of their business colleagues. Her chest squeezed tight. It explained why Zane had left just when they had seemed to be getting somewhere.

"It's beautiful." Everything she could ever have wanted and more, but it was nothing compared to the real treasure Zane was offering her: his heart.

The hurt that had filled her when she had thought Zane couldn't care for her drained away. Out of self-defense she had clung to the picture the press had painted of him, but it was no more real than the picture they had painted of her.

Zane was everything she had been looking for in a husband and more. "Yes, I'll marry you."

He muttered something rough in Medinian and pulled her

close. "Thank goodness. I don't know what I would have done if you'd refused." He buried his head in her hair. "I love you."

The relief of his husky declaration shuddered through her. She wound her arms around his neck and simply held on. They had been walking toward this moment for two years, both stumbling, both making mistakes.

Zane wrapped her even closer, so tight that for a few seconds she could barely breathe. She didn't care. She was having trouble concentrating on anything but the shattering knowledge that Zane *loved* her.

His hold loosened as he talked in a low husky voice. He had been afraid that he had lost her, that he had finally driven her away with his old fear that she couldn't simply love *him,* that there would be a catch—something to be gained—that she would turn out to be dishonest and manipulative. He could bear anything but that. He had been in a terrible situation, unable to stay away from her, but afraid to be with her and discover that she had an agenda, and it wasn't loving him.

He lifted his head, looked into her eyes and the air seemed to go soft and still. "I love you."

And this time he kissed her.

Epilogue

A year later Zane proudly escorted his wife of ten months to the opening of the Ambrosi Pearl facility on Ambrus.

The ceremony, which was to be followed by champagne and a traditional Medinian celebration, with local food and music, was timed for sunset. The whole idea was that the extended twilight would bathe the new center with its large, modern sculpture of a pearl, with a soft, golden glow to celebrate the homecoming of Ambrosi Pearls. Unfortunately, clouds were interfering with the ambiance.

A large crowd of Atraeus and Ambrosi family were present along with locals, clients and of course the media. Constantine and Sienna were there, happily showing off their dark-eyed, definitely blond baby girl. Unbearably cute, Amber Atraeus had clearly inherited the luminous Ambrosi looks and a good helping of the Atraeus charisma.

Lucas and Carla, who had been married for several months, had just returned from an extended holiday in Europe. Looking happy and relaxed, they hadn't started a family yet, but Zane privately thought it wouldn't be long.

Lilah frowned at the gloomy sky, squeezed his hand and checked her watch. "It's time to start."

Glowing and serene in a soft pink dress, her hair coiled in a loose knot, she stepped up to the podium and welcomed the guests.

After providing a quick history of Ambrosi Pearls, Lilah asked a priest to bless the building then handed the proceedings over to Octavia Ambrosi, the great-aunt of both Sienna and Carla.

The oldest living Ambrosi, Octavia, affectionately known as Via, had been Sebastien Ambrosi's sister. She had lived on Ambrus with Sebastien, seen the destruction of the war and the rift that had torn the Atraeus and Ambrosi families apart when Sophie Atraeus and the bridal jewels had disappeared.

In the moment that Via was helped up to the white satin ribbon strung across the front doors of the center the sun came out from behind a cloud, flooding the island with golden light. With great grace Octavia cut the ribbon.

Later on in the evening, when guests had started to leave by the luxury launches that had been laid on by the Atraeus family, Lilah was surprised when Carla made a beeline for her. Since the tension which had erupted between them over Lilah dating Lucas, they had barely spoken, although that was mostly so now because they lived in different countries.

Carla gave her a quick hug and handed her a battered leather case. "This belonged to Sebastien. Since you and Zane will be living on Ambrus in the refurbished villa, we thought you should have it."

Zane's arm came around Lilah, warm and comforting, as she opened the case. Her eyes filled with tears as she studied the silver christening cup engraved with Sebastien's name.

Carla's expression softened as she looked at the cup. "It's of no great monetary value—"

"How did you know?" Zane said abruptly.

"That Lilah's pregnant?" Carla smiled. "It was an informed guess. You two shouldn't look so happy."

Lilah closed the case and tried to give it back to Carla. "This is a family treasure."

Carla smiled as Lucas joined them, followed by Sienna and Constantine with a sleepy Amber tucked into the crook of his arm. "In case you hadn't noticed, you are family."

* * * * *

COMING NEXT MONTH from Harlequin Desire®
AVAILABLE SEPTEMBER 4, 2012

#2179 UP CLOSE AND PERSONAL
Maureen Child

He's danger. She's home and hearth. So the red-hot affair between a California beauty and an Irish rogue ends too soon. But then he returns, wanting to know what she's been hiding....

#2180 A SILKEN SEDUCTION
The Highest Bidder
Yvonne Lindsay

A hotshot art expert seduces an important collection out of a lonely heiress, but their night of passion quickly leads to pregnancy and a marriage of convenience.

#2181 WHATEVER THE PRICE
Billionaires and Babies
Jules Bennett

A Hollywood director's marriage is on the rocks when he gains custody of his orphaned niece. Now he'll do anything to keep his wife...and the baby she's carrying!

#2182 THE MAID'S DAUGHTER
The Men of Wolff Mountain
Janice Maynard

When this billionaire offers the maid's daughter a job, it leads to an affair that reveals the secrets of his traumatic past.

#2183 THE SHEIKH'S CLAIM
Desert Knights
Olivia Gates

When the woman who ignites his senses becomes the mother of his child, nothing can stop him from laying claim to his heir—and her heart.

#2184 A MAN OF DISTINCTION
Sarah M. Anderson

Returning home for the case of his career, a wealthy Native American lawyer must choose between winning in court and reuniting with the love he left behind—and the child she kept a secret.

You can find more information on upcoming Harlequin® titles, free excerpts and more at www.Harlequin.com.

HDCNM0812

REQUEST YOUR FREE BOOKS!
2 FREE NOVELS PLUS 2 FREE GIFTS!

Harlequin Desire

ALWAYS POWERFUL, PASSIONATE AND PROVOCATIVE

YES! Please send me 2 FREE Harlequin Desire® novels and my 2 FREE gifts (gifts are worth about $10). After receiving them, if I don't wish to receive any more books, I can return the shipping statement marked "cancel." If I don't cancel, I will receive 6 brand-new novels every month and be billed just $4.30 per book in the U.S. or $4.99 per book in Canada. That's a saving of at least 14% off the cover price! It's quite a bargain! Shipping and handling is just 50¢ per book in the U.S. and 75¢ per book in Canada.* I understand that accepting the 2 free books and gifts places me under no obligation to buy anything. I can always return a shipment and cancel at any time. Even if I never buy another book, the two free books and gifts are mine to keep forever.

225/326 HDN FEF3

Name	(PLEASE PRINT)	
Address		Apt. #
City	State/Prov.	Zip/Postal Code

Signature (if under 18, a parent or guardian must sign)

Mail to the **Reader Service:**

IN U.S.A.: P.O. Box 1867, Buffalo, NY 14240-1867
IN CANADA: P.O. Box 609, Fort Erie, Ontario L2A 5X3

Not valid for current subscribers to Harlequin Desire books.

Want to try two free books from another line?
Call 1-800-873-8635 or visit www.ReaderService.com.

* Terms and prices subject to change without notice. Prices do not include applicable taxes. Sales tax applicable in N.Y. Canadian residents will be charged applicable taxes. Offer not valid in Quebec. This offer is limited to one order per household. All orders subject to credit approval. Credit or debit balances in a customer's account(s) may be offset by any other outstanding balance owed by or to the customer. Please allow 4 to 6 weeks for delivery. Offer available while quantities last.

Your Privacy—The Reader Service is committed to protecting your privacy. Our Privacy Policy is available online at www.ReaderService.com or upon request from the Reader Service.

We make a portion of our mailing list available to reputable third parties that offer products we believe may interest you. If you prefer that we not exchange your name with third parties, or if you wish to clarify or modify your communication preferences, please visit us at www.ReaderService.com/consumerchoice or write to us at Reader Service Preference Service, P.O. Box 9062, Buffalo, NY 14269. Include your complete name and address.

Harlequin® *Blaze*™

red-hot reads

This navy lieutenant is about to get a blast from the past…and start thinking about the future.

Joanne Rock

captivates with another installment of

Men Out of Uniform

Five years ago, photojournalist Stephanie Rosen was kidnapped in a foreign country. Now, with her demons firmly behind her she is ready to move on…and to rev up her sex life! There's only one man she wants, friend and old flame, navy lieutenant Daniel Murphy. Their one night of passion years ago still leaves Stephanie breathless, and with Daniel on leave she's determined to give him a homecoming to remember.

FULL SURRENDER

Available this September wherever books are sold!

Enjoy this sneak peek of USA TODAY *bestselling author*
Maureen Child's newest title
UP CLOSE AND PERSONAL

Available September 2012 from Harlequin® Desire!

"**L**aura, I know you're in there!"

Ronan Connolly pounded on the bright blue front door, then paused to listen. Not a sound from inside the house, though he knew too well that Laura was in there. Hell, he could practically *feel* her standing just on the other side of the damned door.

He glanced at her car parked alongside the house, then glared again at the still-closed front door.

"You won't convince me you're not at home. Your car is parked in the street, Laura."

Her voice came then, muffled but clear. "It's a driveway in America, Ronan. You're not in Ireland, remember?"

"More's the pity." He scrubbed one hand across his face and rolled his eyes in frustration. If they were in Ireland right now, he'd have half the village of Dunley on his side and he'd bloody well get her to open the door.

"I heard that," she said.

Grinding his teeth together, he counted to ten. Then did it a second time. "Whatever the hell you want to call it, Laura, your car is *here* and so are you. Why not open the door and we can talk this out. Together. In private."

"I've got nothing to say to you."

He laughed shortly. That would be a first indeed, he told himself. A more opinionated woman he had never met. He had to admit, he had enjoyed verbally sparring with her. He admired a quick mind and a sharp tongue. He'd admired her even more once he'd gotten her into his bed.

He glanced down at the dozen red roses he held clutched in his right hand and called himself a damned fool for thinking this woman would be swayed by pretty flowers and a smooth speech. Hell, she hadn't even *seen* the flowers yet. At this rate, she never would.

Huffing out an impatient breath, he lowered his voice. "You know why I'm here. Let's get it done and have it over then."

There was a moment's pause, as if she were thinking about what he'd said. Then she spoke up again. "You can't have him."

"What?"

"You heard me."

Ronan narrowed his gaze fiercely on the door as if he could see through the panel to the woman beyond. "Aye, I heard you. Though, I don't believe it. I've come for what's mine, Laura, and I'm not leaving until I have it."

Will Ronan get what he's come for?

Find out in Maureen Child's new title
UP CLOSE AND PERSONAL

Available September 2012 from Harlequin® Desire!

Harlequin and Mills & Boon are joining forces in a global search for new authors.

In September 2012 we're launching our biggest contest yet—with the prize of being published by the world's leader in romance fiction!

Look for more information on our website, **www.soyouthinkyoucanwrite.com**

So you think you can write? Show us!